PURPLE SKIES OVER SAGE CANYON

By

Kenneth Lee McGee

For The Overland
Adventurers
Who Inspired This Story.

… and especially my friend, Bill.

I would like to thank everyone

who has taken time to visit my website

or my Amazon author page.

I appreciate the support

and kind words.

Thank you Rebecca Carr

for the cover photo.

Sarah Lemmert did an awesome job

with the illustration.

It is exactly the way the character

would have drawn it.

Piqua Mesa

Lake Hiram

Disappointment Creek

Sage Canyon

Piqua Mesa

Piqua Mesa

Chapter One

I stood two feet from the craggy edge of Piqua Mesa, leaned over and nervously stared into the canyon a thousand feet below. I couldn't summon the courage to move closer. From here I could see the faint line marking the switchbacks leading to the verdant landscape. I straightened up, took three steps back and gazed at the menacing purple clouds to the west.

"Bandit, I don't like the color of the sky, or the clouds coming at us."

My five-year-old black lab chose that moment to mark his territory on a nearby rock. Then he moved to the very edge of the mesa and barked at a Red-Tailed hawk soaring overhead.

"Bandit, I don't admit fear to many people, but you'll keep my secret, won't you?"

He tilted his head back and forth as if undecided.

"Be that way. We could head ten miles north to a dirt road leading down, but I am real curious about this canyon. I think it would be worth exploring."

I moved farther away from the edge to study the clouds and marveled at the light show while I finished my second cup of morning coffee. Even at this distance, I could smell the rain and ozone.

The storm was far enough away the thunder was no louder than the sound of the pebble I threw hitting a boulder and bouncing away.

"Get out of here!"

Bandit barked several times.

The scorpion, which was the reason I threw the rock, disappeared under a slab of sandstone.

"Bandit, I thought scorpions only came out at night. Must be why I haven't seen any lately."

Bandit sniffed at the rock but quickly backed away.

It was then I noticed the figure carved into the three-foot tall stone. Though crude, it resembled a bison.

"What do you think about this rock art, Bandit?"

He expressed his disinterest by rolling in the dirt.

Piqua Mesa, when seen from afar, or high above, appeared flat and featureless. Scrub brush, a variety of cactus, boulders, and red dust, which worked its way into every crevice of the Jeep and my clothes, dominated the parched landscape. The faint trail across the mesa top was hard-packed dirt when it wasn't paved with sharp-edged rocks waiting to shred a tire.

I took out my binoculars, turned my St. Louis Cardinals cap backwards, studied the storm again and said, "Bandit, we aren't going to stay up here again tonight. That's for sure."

I had arrived in this part of the Utah desert by following national forest and BLM dirt roads from Coshoctin Grove, where I filled the Jeep and my RotopaX with fuel and bought the last two loaves of bread in the quaint general store. The price of the generic peanut butter caused me to grimace, but I tossed it into my basket anyway.

That was five days ago. I was now fifty-five miles away, as the desert hawk flies. And no one knew I was here.

I traced the dirt road down the mesa until I lost it in the green valley. By sweeping the binoculars back and forth I picked up the sliver of exposed red dirt marking the trail. I followed it to a copse of stunted cottonwoods.

"There is a small clearing, and there might be water in the stream even though it's July. I don't like to stay near a riverbed if there's a chance of rain, but we are too exposed up here."

Bandit moved next to me, and I scratched his ear.

"Storms don't bother you as much anymore, but they sure did when you were a puppy."

I put the binoculars away and walked back to my modified Wrangler Rubicon. Bandit stayed close, but out of sight, as I packed up camp. I shook the water jug I had used earlier and estimated it to be half full. That, and the other two five-gallon containers, would last until I could resupply.

I heard a faint rumble and glanced over my shoulder. A mixture of deep maroon clouds now swirled with the purple ones I spotted earlier, and the chainless wind shrieked through the canyon. I whistled for Bandit, and he charged through the scrub brush and waited until I opened the door. I let him in and made one last check of camp. I walked around the Jeep, tightened the straps on the rooftop tent, wiped the dust from the rear window and vowed to find a car wash soon.

"Are you ready to hit the trail?" I asked Bandit. "We're here to explore, and this canyon looks different. We might find something interesting."

His wagging tail thumped against the passenger seat at a heavy metal tempo.

I placed my cell phone in the holder mounted on the dash and checked for a signal.

"No bars out here. Didn't really expect any. I have my satellite phone in case I need it."

I turned on my tablet, opened the offline map for the area and looked for a road leading out of the canyon. The oval-shaped canyon angled slightly southwest at one point. My map didn't display a road, but I wasn't concerned. I had been in other areas where the maps didn't disclose a primitive trail.

"The canyon appears to be ten miles long. Give or take. The map shows a short side canyon, but no road in it either."

Bandit tilted his head and stared at me.

"Okay, you don't care. The trail to the top of Piqua Mesa was no picnic. It might have been frequently traveled at one time, but I doubt anyone has used it in the last year, or longer. I didn't see any tire tracks in the dirt sections. If we backtrack, it would add too many miles to our trip, and it's just slightly better than going ahead."

I fired up the Jeep, listened to the gears grind as I shifted into 4Low and headed to the point where the edge of the mesa opened to a small crack barely wider than the Jeep and uncomfortably off camber. This would be my trail going down. I had walked part of it the day before, and the thought of driving down it made my hands sweat and my heart race. The trail looked as though it had never been graded and was covered with loose rocks in places. At least there was a bit more room at the switchbacks.

"There's no turning back now, Bandit." I took a deep breath then flipped on all my lights even though it was mid-morning. I dropped ten feet down the crack, made a hard right turn and narrowly avoided scraping the side of the Wrangler. The shelf road hugging the cliff most likely started out as a horse trail, or possibly, a narrow cattle trail. I settled in for a three or four mile drive that could take as long as three hours unless the trail improved closer to the canyon floor. It would save backtracking across the mesa.

When I could see the western sky, it appeared more menacing than before. I couldn't drive faster for fear of damaging the Jeep, or making an error in tire placement and courting disaster. I reached the third switchback and stopped.

"I wish you could be my spotter, Bandit. This one is tighter than the others, and that boulder is just close enough to be in the way. Stay here while I check it out."

He put his front paws on the dash and stared out the windshield. I edged along the Jeep with two feet between me and the vertical drop to the lower switchback.

"Great! Now the wind decides to pick up."

I walked through the switchback, and, even with my limited experience, I knew this would require a three-point turn. Maybe a five-point turn.

Five minutes later, I was past the switchback, which proved to be the most difficult. The trail widened slightly, though sections were off camber. At one point the trail narrowed again, and I felt the Jeep slide toward the edge on the loose rocks. My front passenger tire slipped into a hole, and I heard rocks and dirt tumbling over the edge.

"This doesn't look good," I said to Bandit as the Jeep started to slide again. I stabbed the accelerator with my right foot. The Jeep lurched forward and rocked side to side as the tires struggled for grip. The passenger tire climbed out of the hole. I floored the gas pedal. The rear tire hit the hole, bounced up and the Jeep shot forward. I slammed on the brakes and Bandit tumbled into the footwell. I closed my eyes and waited for the Jeep to slide over the edge. When the Jeep stopped rocking, I threw it in park, set the emergency brake and waited for my heart to stop racing. Then I got out. There was barely room for me to wriggle past the Jeep along the sheer rock wall. I stood at the back and inspected the hole. Then I looked up the vertical wall. Bandit was sitting on the driver's seat with his nose out the partially opened window.

"There are stains on the wall. It must be a waterfall at times, and it crosses the trail and erodes it even more."

I got back in the Jeep and took another look at my map as I drank a bottle of water.

"I know this is taking longer than expected, but I'd rather take it easy than risk making a mistake."

Bandit curled up on the passenger seat.

We reached the canyon floor an hour later without further incident.

"I feel better now. How about you?"

Bandit barked once and wagged his tail. I found the small clearing within five minutes, parked the Jeep in the nearly-level area and we hopped out. The faint sound of water beyond the trees pleased my ears. I could now see the canyon floor sloped gradually to the west and the walls rose straighter and higher. I looked back at the trail I had descended, shook my head and then stared at the vertical walls.

"I can't say for sure, Bandit, but that might have been the only place in this canyon where a trail was even possible. I doubt the road will be passable much longer." I pointed to my right. "Those cliffs are straighter than the ruler the nuns used to smack students who weren't paying attention." I flexed my fingers and waited for a reaction. "I guess you don't get my sense of humor, huh?"

We jumped back into the Jeep as the angry, purple sky opened up. The lightning flashed. The thunder reverberated off the cliffs in a never-ending cacophony of eardrum-shattering echoes. The heavy drops of rain splattered and mixed with the layer of dust on the Jeep turning it to a sticky, red mud.

"If we're lucky, the rain will clean the Jeep."

Ten minutes later, the sky matched the original color of my Jeep, and the parched ground had absorbed every drop of rain. The stream gurgled over its rock-strewn path with renewed vigor, and I noticed a thin waterfall at the southeastern end of the canyon.

Even though the sun was beating directly down, I decided to explore the shaded area along the creek. A light breeze evaporated my sweat instantly. I wrapped my red bandana around my neck and felt the residual effects of the sunburn from three days earlier. Bandit raced ahead and would occasionally double back to make sure I was still following him. Birds squawked to announce the presence of a new predator.

"Bandit, you might have difficulty catching a bird, but I wouldn't be surprised if you find plenty of rabbits or other small game to hunt."

I shielded my eyes from the sun and gazed at the thousand foot wall to my left. I spotted a ledge approximately two hundred feet up, and saw the remains of a cliff dwelling. When I saw something reach out, I staggered back, tripped over a rock and landed on my butt on top of a cactus. I yelled involuntarily. Though more than my dignity was injured, I continued to stare at the ruin. I realized the thing I saw was an arm and a hand holding something.

The hand's owner dropped the white object. I watched it smack into the detritus fifty feet away, bounce into the sky, roll down the slope, and end up in four pieces, fifteen feet away. I shuddered when I realized I was looking at pieces of a human skull.

Chapter Two

>

I couldn't move. My muscles were paralyzed despite the sharp cactus needles digging into my flesh. Bandit barked at the object and raced back and forth stirring up the red dirt. After staring at the pieces for five seconds, which felt like an eternity, I lifted my eyes to the cliff dwelling. The sun blurred my vision, but I thought I was looking at a white bear. Then it waved.

"Hello the canyon floor! I say hello! Do you see my artifact?"

I knew bears couldn't talk and realized I was looking at a man with a full white beard and stringy hair hanging to his shoulders.

The strange-looking man cupped his hands to his mouth and hollered, "Hello! Can you hear me?"

I grimaced as I stood. I waved but had no voice to reply, so I pointed. Bandit approached the largest part of the skull and growled menacingly.

"Stay there. I will be right down."

He disappeared, but then emerged from behind the partial wall. His tangled white hair flowed onto his white shirt. He made his way, as nimbly as a mountain goat, along an unseen path. He disappeared again for a couple minutes, and I thought he might have been a figment of my imagination until I saw the skull again.

"That thing is staring at me, Bandit."

Bandit darted back and forth while barking.

The white-haired man was at the base of the canyon wall when he reappeared and approached.

I backed away, pointed to his artifact and asked, "Who are you? Is that what I think it is? Where did you find it?"

He rushed down the talus slope to the broken pieces, gathered them and attempted to put them back together.

"Bandit! Quiet!" I ordered.

"You startled me with your scream," he said, finally looking at me.

"Not as much as you scared the crap out of me. Who are you?" I repeated.

"Oh, forgive my lack of manners." He held his artifact in his left hand and offered his right.

I backed farther away, holding up my hands. "We can dispense with the pleasantries for now."

"I am Dr. Hiram Hirschfield, the retired chair of the St. Stephen's University archaeology department in Bozeman. I discovered this site forty years ago and have been researching it ever since."

My finger trembled as I pointed to the skull fragments.

"Oh, this old thing. It's nothing."

"It looks human."

He tilted his head and peered at the pieces. "It is human, but it didn't originate from here. I brought it with so I could compare it to the one I found last month."

I gulped, coughed and asked, "You found a skull up there?"

"A skull and several other bones. Not quite a complete skeleton." He stared at me. "Who are you? I assume you are the owner of that Jeep, correct?"

"Yes, it is my Jeep. I'm Rhett Carter. I camped on top of the mesa last night, but I came down here to avoid the storm. This is BLM land."

He waved dismissively. "You aren't trespassing or anything. I haven't seen another person..." He gestured to the cliff dwelling. "A flesh and bone human in the last ten years I've been researching this canyon except for..."

"Have you been here for ten years?" I believed it possible because of his appearance.

He chuckled and answered, "Not continuously. That was quite a storm, huh?"

"Yes, but it didn't last long."

"They never do. They make a loud racket though." He waved his hands in an exaggerated manner. "Sounds like bombs exploding."

I looked around. "This canyon is beautiful. I would have thought people explore it all the time."

By now Bandit decided the professor was not a threat, stood next to him and sniffed his hand.

"It is, but accessibility is the issue. The entrance from the west has been blocked by a landslide for years. A storm last month washed it out even more. There is a slot at the southern end of the side canyon." He pointed in that direction. "But the entrance is impossible to find unless you know what to look for. You would need a team of skillful climbers to gain access to Sage Canyon from the top of the mesa."

He turned in a circle as he talked in short bursts. "There are no trails to descend. Not even one for mountain goats. Believe me I've searched. That leaves only one possibility."

"Wait! This isn't Serotta Canyon?"

"No. Serotta is ten miles northeast of here. Some maps might label this Serotta, but the correct name is Sage Canyon."

I didn't understand the reasoning behind the name because the canyon was grassy unlike the sage-covered mesa tops. I pointed to Piqua Mesa. "I descended along an old trail."

"I assumed as much." He looked skyward and shook his head. "Astounding! No one has used that old trail for decades. Not in a vehicle anyway. It's difficult for a horse to descend. How did you get past the leaning rock?"

I shrugged. "I don't know what you're talking about."

He moved closer and pointed to a spot about halfway down the cliff. "There used to be a slab leaning against the wall. A man on a horse could squeeze under it, but no motorized vehicle could pass." He rubbed his beard, and I saw a puff of dust.

"It must not be there anymore. I only had trouble at one switchback."

"Makes no difference. You can't go back up. Not even in your fancy rig. It's too steep."

"I wasn't about to attempt it. Some sections of the trail were so off camber, I thought I would roll the Jeep."

17

"You're stuck here with me."

"Why? I don't understand. How did you get here?"

He turned toward the opposite end of the canyon. "I know where to find the slot canyon entrance." He pointed to the south. "Piqua Mesa narrows to less than a mile wide, and is even narrower by the side canyon. It doesn't have an official name, but I call it Escape Canyon. The land on the other side of Piqua Mesa is more inaccessible than the Maze."

"Canyonland's Maze?"

He nodded, and set the pieces of skull on a boulder.

"I've been on top of Island In The Sky, and checked out the Needles district, but I avoided the Maze."

"I explored it years ago."

I pointed to the western end of the valley. "Will someone fix the road?"

"Eventually, but not this year. It wasn't really a road before. Just a wide horse trail. Your Jeep might not fit. I would use an ATV in prior years."

"Do you live in there?" I pointed to the cliff dwelling.

"At times. It looks like an abandoned ruin, but it's livable inside. I get up and down using the footholds Native Americans carved in the crack, but it's getting more difficult because of my age... and weight." He glanced around as if someone might be lurking nearby to eavesdrop and whispered, "This canyon is haunted."

I expressed my disbelief with a snort.

"Have you ever heard of Zenus Sage?"

I shook my head.

"According to legend, he prospected in this part of Utah before any other white men arrived. He left and rode into Independence, Missouri, around 1810, or so, with pelts and hides to trade. He got drunk and claimed to have found gold and silver. No one believed him. He bought some mining gear and headed back."

"Is this canyon named for him?"

Dr. Hirschfield nodded then put his hand to his ear. "Do you hear that?"

"What?" I turned to face the side of Piqua Mesa just as part of the wall collapsed.

We stood immobile until the dust forced us to seek shelter behind a large boulder.

"No one will ever climb Piqua Mesa using that trail again." I slapped my baseball cap against my thigh then coughed several times.

"I hope you have enough food to last a while."

"I do, and I'm willing to share until help arrives. I could call the authorities to inform them of the collapse."

"Cell phones don't normally work in here."

"Don't need one. I have a sat-phone."

"Good. No one expects me back for two months."

"You mentioned a skull up there." I pointed to the ledge.

"Ah, indeed. If the legend is true, this canyon is the site of Zenus Sage's lost treasure. The myth is he returned to his claim, worked the mine for a time and hauled enough ore out of the canyon to make a fortune."

19

"No way." I shook my head. "Unless he used burros."

"Probably. Supposedly, men tried to follow him here, but he evaded them." He leaned closer and whispered, "I don't believe a word of it."

"No gold or silver, huh?"

He chuckled and said, "I believe that part, but I don't think the gold and silver ever left this canyon."

"Why not?"

"No historical evidence of Sage ever becoming a rich man."

"Maybe he worked the mine..." I shrugged. I had no clue what might have happened.

"There's no evidence of a mine anywhere."

I looked at the canyon walls. "I doubt if I could spot a mine unless it was a large undertaking."

"The legend claims he went insane and died of starvation."

"Are you saying the bones up there belong to... whatever his name was?"

"Zenus Sage." He clapped a meaty hand on my shoulder. "My boy, you could be standing on a fortune. The only catch is you might not live long enough to find it."

Chapter Three

I backed away as if he might attack me with a weapon. "Why would you say such a thing? Are we in danger?"

The Professor, as I thought of him, clasped his arms over his chest, looked up at the rim of the canyon in all directions, then nodded. "Many strange, unexplained incidents have occurred through the years. Perhaps more frequently the last couple years. The canyon has always had a mystery about it. I've often felt like someone was watching from up there." He lifted his eyes to the rim again.

For a split-second, I saw the shadow of fear cross his eyes. Then he blinked and the feeling disappeared. I looked across to where the dust was still settling on the debris from the latest landslide.

"Does that happen often?"

"I've witnessed three major rock slides in the last forty years. I've heard others. Geologists have a name for this kind of rock."

"What do they call it?"

He grinned and answered, "Rotten."

I fell for his joke and watched him shake with laughter.

"You may, or may not, have felt a tremor moments ago."

I shook my head. "I felt nothing."

He tilted his hand back and forth. "They happen more than we realize. This causes the rock to weaken over time. Geologic time." He shrugged and added, "Eventually, the canyon walls will collapse, and we can walk out of here."

"How soon?"

He rubbed his beard thoughtfully, and again I noticed the puff of dust. "Well, if we live to be a million, I imagine we could walk right out. A stroll in the desert."

I listened again to his hearty laugh and watched his ample stomach shake. Then I stared at my Jeep. "If it had happened yesterday..." I shook my head.

"If can be a powerful word. Don't let it consume you."

I looked up. "I didn't realize Piqua Mesa was so large."

"I don't know the exact size in acres, or square miles, but it is one of the largest in the state."

"Sage Canyon is different than the last canyon I explored. It's lush and green like an oasis."

"The mesa is large enough, and the canyon small enough to have gone unnoticed and unexplored for thousands of years."

"Did the stream create the canyon?"

"Partially. If I had to guess, I would say an earthquake split the mesa first and then over time the two sections," he rubbed his hands together, "were drawn close together then the river separated them again."

"It's certainly not the Grand Canyon, but it looks more habitable."

He waved a hand to include the entire canyon. "This area was one of the last blank spots on the map. The natives had a name for it, but it wasn't called Piqua Mesa until the early 20th century." He chuckled and added, "Sage Canyon wasn't rediscovered by white men until 1860, or thereabouts."

"The Zenus Sage you mentioned earlier discovered it first, right?"

"Quite likely," the professor said. "On early maps, the mesa was depicted as one solid plateau."

"So no one knew Sage Canyon existed, right?"

He nodded. "A few people knew about it, but it wasn't added to most maps until men could fly. Piqua Mesa has been uninhabited for hundreds of years. No water and little vegetation suitable for cattle."

"I knew the canyon existed because of my maps, but it was rather deceptive. I was exploring a trail in the Jeep and didn't see it until I was almost to the edge. I had to slam on the brakes even though I was crawling like a turtle."

Bandit heard something in the grass and began to hunt.

"What do we do now? If what you're telling me is true, my Jeep and I are trapped. There's no way out."

"You and I could leave through the slot canyon," he replied. "But it will be a while before you can drive your Jeep out of Sage Canyon. Remind me to show you the remains of another vehicle someday." He pointed to the far end of the canyon. "It takes several hours to reach it."

"We could drive."

"Only part of the way. What trail might have existed years ago, has long since returned to nature. We will follow game trails."

"You refer to the roads as trails. Why?"

"Force of habit, I suppose."

I couldn't see Bandit, but I could hear him occasionally. I knew he wouldn't stray too far. I shifted my weight back and forth and tried to think of a way out of the canyon.

"It's about time for lunch. Care to join me?"

I stared at the professor then asked, "Where? Is there a McDonald's nearby?"

He laughed and pointed up the slope in the direction he had emerged earlier. "Allow me to give you a tour."

"Okay, but I have a small kitchen setup in the Jeep. I have food in the fridge."

He stared at the Jeep. "Astounding! Who would have ever thought it possible."

He headed up the slope. I listened for Bandit, but didn't hear him. I followed the professor until he disappeared. I peered at the place I had last seen him. It was twenty feet away, and didn't appear any different than the rest of the canyon walls. After a moment, he reemerged.

"You disappeared. I glanced away, and you vanished like a ghost."

"Sorry. I should have mentioned my luxury quarters." He laughed heartily. "Please follow me."

I made my way up the last stretch of slope. The rocks were smaller and looser here. For every two feet I climbed, I slid down one. I reached the wall and, to my utter amazement, found a gap of two or three feet between the outer section and the inner. I slipped inside and gazed upward. I could see a narrow ribbon of blue sky a thousand feet above me.

"There are natural shelves and steps carved into the crack all the way to the top. I know from experience."

"You climbed out through here?"

"A long time ago." He patted his stomach. "I wouldn't fit now even if I had the stamina to make the climb."

When my eyes adjusted to the dim light, I could see part of a cave. I moved closer and could see a fire ring and a small cot tucked into the corner.

"This is where I usually spend my nights. There is enough ventilation for the smoke to escape."

I saw a stack of firewood against one wall. "Do you stay here in winter?"

"I have."

"Why were you on the ledge during the storm?" I moved around the *cave* and saw a shelf holding supplies. There were cans of soup, vegetables, baked beans and even canned meat. I faced him and waited for an answer.

He shrugged. "I should have known better. The storms occur in the afternoon, but I was so interested in comparing the skulls, I lost track of time."

"Do you honestly believe the skeleton is the old miner?"

"I do, but I have no way to prove it. I haven't been able to track down any ancestors to do a DNA comparison. The bloodline of Zenus Sage ended with his death."

Bandit scurried into the cave gently carrying a rabbit in his mouth.

"Ah! I like this," the professor said, rubbing his hands together. "We have a natural hunter living with us. There is an abundant supply of small game in the valley. There are no large predators left. I saw a mountain lion several years ago, but nothing since."

We decided to have rabbit stew for dinner, but I persuaded him to share lunch with me at the Jeep. I needed to set out my solar panels to keep the batteries charged. I planned to conserve my gasoline since I might be here indefinitely. I opened the back of the Jeep and showed him my rig. He was impressed by how I could pack so much gear into the small space. Since I needed to use the bread, we sat in my camp chairs and ate peanut butter sandwiches.

"I haven't eaten peanut butter in months. This is tasty, quick and filling."

After lunch he offered to take me up to the cliff dwelling. I looked up, thought about it, but said, "Maybe we can save that for later. I'd like to explore more of the canyon floor. Does this creek run the whole length? Is there water all year round? I'm sorry to badger you with so many questions."

"I'm glad for the company. I've been alone all summer."

He got up, walked closer to the creek and gestured to the west. "I've only seen it dry a couple times." He did a 180 and pointed to the waterfall, which by now was a mere trickle compared to after the storm, and explained, "There is a natural spring up there. I've never been able to find the source, but it's a good source of clean water."

I shielded my eyes and stared at the rock face, but it became a blur in the shade.

"If you follow the creek west, you will reach a small pond, lake, whatever."

He became rather animated as he talked about the life-sustaining source of water. I watched and listened with amazement as he described the creek.

"How many waterfalls are there?"

"If you only count the ones three feet high or more," he paused for a moment, and I could see him picturing the falls in his mind. "Six when the water is at its lowest level. There is a trail alongside it for most of the way. In some places the trails veers away, but you are always nearby."

"Would you mind if Bandit and I take time to explore?"

"Go ahead. I need to work on my journal, and I usually take a nap. It's too hot to work in the mid-afternoon."

I cleaned up after our simple lunch. I left the camp chairs out because, after all, who was going to steal them. I whistled for Bandit. He appeared within a few seconds. "We're going for a walk." He understood and wagged his tail.

I grabbed a bottle of water and debated whether to take my backpack or not.

"What do you think, Bandit? Should I bring it?"

He raced away, but returned seconds later.

"You're in a hurry to get going."

I decided to leave it behind. Out of habit, I locked the Jeep. I took a few steps away, and stopped. I heard the professor chuckle.

"Old habit," I said.

"People say I have an honest face." He laughed and added, "At least the part they can see."

I unlocked it, opened the door and tossed the key fob inside. I waved to the professor, adjusted my cap and began my first hike in Sage Canyon.

Chapter Four

⌐

"Bandit, you may not understand, but, in a way, I feel like Robinson Crusoe or Tom Hank's character in *Castaway*. At least we have company."

He trotted beside me as we walked down the middle of the *trail*, as the professor would call it. The Jeep would have no trouble navigating the road. So far. The dirt was hard-packed and the rocks were not large enough to cause a problem. I came across several ledges, none of them over three feet high, which the Jeep could easily descend. I kept turning my head from one side of the canyon to the other always gazing upward trying to determine if the cliffs on one side of the canyon were taller than the other. I tripped over a rock, nearly fell, but regained my balance in time.

"Bandit, you need to remind me to watch where I'm going. Can you do that for me?"

He barked and raced ahead, veering off the trail. He returned and splashed through the creek to the other side. I wasn't worried about either of us getting lost as long as I could hear the creek.

After studying the cliffs for several minutes, I came to the conclusion they were close to the same height. There were dips and rises on both sides. I saw a few trees growing out of the side of the cliff. I was amazed how they could find a foothold and grow out of what I assumed to be solid rock.

The trail would narrow at times, though never to the point where the Jeep wouldn't fit. After hiking for an hour, or so, I left the main trail and decided to investigate a path leading to the south wall. I thought I spotted an opening which might possibly be the road leading out of Sage Canyon. I was still questioning the professor's comment about there not being a way out of the canyon. I wanted to either validate his statement, or disprove it. I climbed the slope, always gazing upward, shielding my eyes from the sun, and peering into the shadows.

"No luck, Bandit. The light plays tricks on my eyes. What I thought might be an opening was merely a shadow."

I went back to the road and within a hundred feet, it edged closer to the creek. I could hear a rushing sound, and soon found the first waterfall. I stood at the edge of the creek and peered into the deep chasm. All four feet of it.

"Well, Bandit, the professor did say the waterfalls were a minimum of three feet high."

Bandit searched for food in the clear water.

"I forgot to ask him if this creek has a name. If it doesn't, I think I will name it Disappointment Creek because the waterfalls are lacking in height."

By now the creek was almost in the middle of the canyon, and it was much straighter than back at the Jeep. This was because the ground was dipping. I knew a waterway would meander on level ground. The cliffs were noticeably higher on both sides now, and still appeared to be as smooth as glass.

The road crossed the creek for the first time. It would cross it a dozen times in total. I hiked up the slope as far as I could to inspect the north wall. There appeared to be more flora on this side. I assumed it was because of more exposure to sunlight, but not being a biologist, this was only a guess.

"Bandit! Where are you, boy?"

I hadn't seen, or heard, him for several minutes. When he didn't appear, I whistled. I crossed the creek and looked downstream. I spotted Bandit sitting low in the grass watching four deer. The wind was coming toward me, so I didn't think the deer could sense my presence. I stood still and watched as they drank their fill from the creek. I stepped on a rock, and the deer fled. Bandit turned to me, and was probably upset because I had spooked his prey. I'm not sure if he had ever seen a deer. He certainly couldn't bring one down. Rabbits were his usual choice.

I could hear another waterfall. This one was the largest I found out later. The creek, now divided into three forks, channels, whatever, dropped eight to ten feet in a series of small falls before coming back together.

An hour later I stood at the edge of the lake. It was too large to call it a pond. Eyesight showed me the creek fed into the lake and common sense told me it must leave the lake somewhere. I walked around the north shore. Upon reaching the cliff, I climbed to a narrow shelf ten feet above the water. I needed a break, so I sat on the ledge with my feet dangling in space. I finished the bottle of water and wished I had another one.

"Bandit! Where are you hunting now?"

I heard him scampering through the brush, and a few seconds later, he joined me.

"Can you see the fish?" I pointed to the lake. "The water is so clear. If I had a pole, I could catch some for dinner. Maybe you will learn how to fish. I should ask the professor if he fishes when we get back."

I saw evidence of the water covering the ledge. It wasn't quite a bathtub ring, but there were differences in the color of the rocks. I followed another ledge to the south shore and finished my exploration of the lake. I had heard of rivers and creeks disappearing underground and assumed this must be the case here.

"The spring runoff must increase its size."

I realized Bandit wasn't listening, left the lake and made my way to the lone side canyon. I searched for the slot the professor used to gain access, but without luck. He might have disguised it, and would need to show me the entrance. I returned to the main canyon and compared the western wall to those on the north and south. This wall was not as vertical though it appeared to be just as high. I thought it might be possible to find a route out of the canyon. I searched for a sign of the trail. I couldn't be sure, but I thought I could trace sections up the cliff.

The sun was setting, so I called for Bandit and we headed back. I tried to stay on the opposite side of the creek as I returned. We saw more deer. They didn't fear us, but appeared curious. They would watch and, as long as Bandit didn't startle them, they went about their business without any regard to us.

"Bandit, I know you're thinking of the deer as a meal, but you might need my help. You are an excellent hunter, but I don't think you can catch one on your own."

He stayed behind to watch the deer as I moved on. Eventually, they scattered and he raced to catch up.

I angled closer to the north wall and found less debris at the base of the cliffs. I wasn't sure why this was the case, but the hiking was easier away from the valley floor where the thick flora hindered progress. By the time I neared camp, my stomach grumbled from hunger, and I craved a bottle of water to slake my thirst. I was about a quarter mile from the Jeep, still following the base of the cliff approximately twenty-five feet above the canyon floor, when I found myself stranded on a ledge with no apparent way down. I couldn't continue because a landslide had created a gap of twenty feet. I searched in vain for a way to scramble onto the boulders below.

"Bandit, as much as I hate to say it, we need to retrace our steps."

He didn't seem to mind. He had been drinking from the creek all afternoon, and might have found a tasty critter to consume, also. Backtracking and hiking back to camp took close to an hour. I could smell dinner, but needed to stop at the Jeep first. I would ask the professor later how, and where, he relieved himself. I didn't want to drag my cassette toilet with me on my hikes.

Chapter Five

Bandit could smell the rabbit stew as we got close to *base camp*, as I decided to call it. He dashed ahead, and I stopped at the Jeep to grab more water. I fished an energy bar out of the backpack and chuckled. I should have taken it along. The shadows made it difficult to locate the cave even though I had been there earlier. I made my way up the slope and heard the professor talking to Bandit. I slipped into the crack, and they turned to face me.

"Ah! You made it back. How was your adventure?"

"Tiring, but extremely interesting." I sat on one of the large boulders placed around the fire ring. He expected to hear more, but I was too exhausted, mentally and physically, to talk.

Once he realized I was not in the mood for a conversation, he said, "The stew is ready. It's rather simple. I don't add a lot of spice other than salt and pepper. I did make a few biscuits."

I glanced up at him from my rock.

"I have the basics. Flour, sugar, coffee. I used to smoke years ago, but I gave it up. Bad for your health, I hear."

I was too tired to laugh at his humor.

"The biscuits are dry, and I don't have butter. No cows in the canyon anymore. That I know of, at least."

I smiled but hoped he wouldn't be a garrulous companion. He sensed my reticence, so we ate our meal with a minimum of conversation.

"I saved some of the rabbit for Bandit."

"He will appreciate it. I don't often give him people food."

I caved and gave half of my second biscuit to Bandit. Between the biscuit and the rabbit, he was satisfied. I helped clean up, and we started a fire even though it was still in the upper 70s.

"What can you tell me about Sage Canyon?" I hoped to get the professor talking, so he wouldn't ask about my life.

The professor stroked his beard. I didn't see the puff of dust this time. He added a larger log to the fire and sat back.

"I could tell you about the geology..."

I grimaced and shook my head.

"The history?"

I nodded. Bandit lay next to me and promptly fell asleep. I was determined to stay awake and listen.

"Native Americans were, of course, the first to discover and settle the canyon. There are petroglyphs and pictographs all along the lower walls. Some have been dated at over 800 years..."

The professor sensed I wasn't interested in ancient rock art, so he switched to more modern history.

"How about this? The first white men known to do anything in the canyon, other than Zenus Sage, were the Hough brothers. Bill and David."

"Now I'm interested."

"In the 1870s they ran cattle in the canyons around here. They were the ones who discovered the trail down Piqua Mesa and expanded it using simple hand tools. No dynamite."

"I could see pickaxe marks on the wall as I descended."

"The valley could support a thousand head or more. Plenty of water and grass."

"I couldn't help notice the variety of flora. I could see the grass from on top the mesa, but there are several types of cactus, too."

"It is rather unique, and I questioned a colleague about it. He rattled off some technical jargon while I nodded and thought about fossils. The grass has taken over in many places, and there aren't as many cacti as years ago. My guess would be the stream has become more dependable over the years."

"Tell me more about the brothers."

"I believe they lived in the area until the 1890s. By then they had moved on from raising cattle in the canyon." He waved his hands. "Can you imagine leading all those cows down that trail? And!" He waved again. "They did it all by themselves. Two cowboys. Of course, once the cattle was in the valley, there was nowhere for them to go." He paused again and asked, "There was one great advantage. Can you think of it?"

I thought for a moment then shook my head.

"Take a guess."

I shrugged.

"No rustlers!"

"I get it now."

"No rustler would make the effort to rustle cattle from down here. There were too many other herds much easier to steal. Outlaws would use Utah canyons for hideouts, but I've never seen any evidence, or heard any rumors, of anyone using this canyon for that purpose. The Indians... I mean Native Americans..."

"You can call them Indians as far as I'm concerned."

"There were many different tribes living in this area in the 1800s. It might have been..."

"The Utes?"

"Ah! Correct. The state is named for them. I believe there were Shoshone and Southern Paiutes in the area. There are several reservations to this day."

"And casinos," I added. "I've stayed overnight in their parking lots when I couldn't find dispersed camping."

"I've never been inside a casino," he admitted.

"Nor have I. Where were you born?"

Everyone, except me, likes to talk about themselves, so I hoped the professor was no exception.

"Ennis City, Montana. February 8, 1943."

"Get out! That would make you 75."

He smiled and nodded. "Yes it does. I lived there until I left for college. St. Stephen's in Bozeman. I met my wife, Effie, there. Graduated, took a job in the history department and never left. I retired ten years ago, and have subsequently spent much time in this canyon."

37

He paused, and I didn't want to ask about his wife, so I asked, "Any children? Grandchildren?"

"Three boys and one girl. They are grown and scattered around the country. Heck! Even the grandchildren are adults. All nine of them."

"Any great-grandchildren?"

"Not yet, but I imagine it will happen soon. Effie would like to have babies in the house again." He waved his hands and chuckled. "Just for a visit. She used to join me on my archaeological adventures, but she broke a hip seven... no eight years ago. It required surgery, but not a hip replacement."

"That must have been painful. I crashed while mountain biking years ago, and fractured my pelvis."

"Now she stays home and takes care of our social media. She allows me to have my eccentricities." He stroked his beard and tugged on his hair. "When I was still teaching, I looked more presentable. In the beginning, at least. Twenty years ago I decided to cultivate my *mountain man* appearance. It's more fitting for an old man who digs for bones, fossils and gold."

"I thought you were a bear at first."

He chuckled and poked the fire with his stick. The flames re-energized.

"I've never seen a bear in here, but I have in Montana, of course. We still live in the same house I bought five years after we married. It was large enough for the family then, but wouldn't hold everyone if they all decided to come for a visit at the same time. That seldom happens, so I won't need to add extra bedrooms."

He rambled on about the university, his many expeditions and the books he had written. Most of which, he confessed, now lie dormant in college libraries covered in dust. He finally ran out of breath, paused and I knew he was about to ask the inevitable question.

"Now that you know all about me, what should I know about you?"

Chapter Six

"I knew you would get around to asking at some point. There isn't a lot to tell."

He smiled and said, "I'm an old man, considered wise by some, son, and I know this for a fact. When a man your age decides to travel the countryside in a Jeep with only a dog for a companion, he has a story to share." He pointed to my hand. "You are wearing a wedding band, but you haven't mentioned a wife. There's a reason, but I will wait for you to tell it."

I twisted the gold band around my finger for a moment. Then I closed my eyes, took a deep breath and responded, "Her name was Noura. She and our son, Reid, were killed three years ago in a traffic accident. A teenage driver was texting and ran a red light. They didn't have a chance. He was driving his parents' large SUV and going over sixty miles an hour. He survived with barely a scratch, but my family was taken from me in an instant." I clenched my jaw and stared at the fluffy clouds passing over the canyon.

"I'm sorry," the professor whispered.

"Reid was ten." I scratched Bandit's ear. "I tried to return to my life too soon. After a year of going through the motions and listening to well wishes from people, I decided to leave. I heard the phrase 'they're in a better place' one too many times."

"People can be so insensitive."

"I sold the house. Oh, the parents of the driver had insurance. We settled out of court. Between selling the house and the insurance settlement, I had enough money to live however I wanted. I chose to live simply and avoid people as much as possible."

After I paused, he asked, "What did you do for a living."

I snorted and replied, "I worked with my father. His father started a law firm. My father joined, and I was expected to follow suite. I did, but my heart was never in it."

The professor nodded. "I was supposed to be a dentist."

"My grandfather, Wilson Johnson Carter, founded the firm, worked a minimum of eighty hours a week, retired at the age of eighty-four and passed away a month later. My father, W. Jackson Carter, expanded the firm and moved the office from South Hampshire to Newcastle, Illinois. We specialized in corporate law and our clients paid exorbitant fees. A sixty hour week was a vacation. The associates worked eighty hours or more. The turnover rate was over fifty percent."

"What does the *W* stand for?"

I chuckled. "Warfield. It's grandmother's maiden name. W. Jackson Carter sounded dignified, and Dad used it in court, but everyone called him Jack socially. My grandmother insisted I be named Warfield, Wilson, or Warren J-something. My mother hated the idea and refused to go along. She and Grandmother reached a compromise without suing each other."

"An accomplishment in today's world."

"Mother loved the Clark Gable character, of course, and she insisted on naming me Rhett. Grandmother settled for a middle name of Warren, and she calls me that to this day purely to aggravate my mother."

"How did you meet your Noura?"

I smiled and said, "In high school. We joined the debate teams, and were on opposite sides of a debate about the economic impact of foreign oil dependence, or something ridiculous like that. I don't remember the exact topic."

"Who won?"

"Oh, I never won an argument against Noura."

The professor laughed. "I can relate. Where did you live?"

"South Hampshire, Illinois. It's forty-five minutes out of Chicago. It's either the third or fourth largest city in the state, I believe. I attended St. Raymond's High School, and she attended The Barclay Academy. Barclay was a private school for families with money. After our first debate, we contacted each other, but didn't date. We became friends. We decided to enroll at Dartmouth because we loved New Hampshire, and it was far from home. We wanted to escape our families' influence. During the summer after our first year, instead of going home, we traveled together. We toured New England, the Atlantic provinces of Canada and fell in love. I asked her to marry me standing on the shore of the Atlantic Ocean in St. John's, Newfoundland. She said yes, by the way."

I liked the professor's easy way of laughing.

"We headed home and told our parents. Mother insisted on a huge wedding. We agreed knowing it would never happen. We lived in an apartment for the next two years of college, and got married before our final year. Noura's parents divorced when she was twelve. She hasn't...Sorry, hadn't... seen her father since the divorce. Her mother remarried but didn't stay in contact. She lives somewhere in Florida. Reid never met either of his maternal grandparents, and he was okay with it. After graduation we headed to law school in New York City."

"Your wife was also an attorney?" he asked.

"She was set to become the next partner in the firm."

I paused, rubbed Bandit's ears for a time. The professor waited patiently for me to continue.

"After the accident, I worked for a year. I hated every minute. Finally, I walked into my father's office, took a seat and told him I was leaving the firm. He tried to talk me out of it, of course. His silver tongue won many arguments in court, but my mind was made up. I sold the house, like I mentioned, received the settlement and rented a cabin in the U.P. I spent time hiking through the woods with Bandit, determined to find a new direction for my life. One day I met a man in town, who was traveling across the country in his Jeep Wrangler. I invited him to the cabin. He accepted, and we talked for most of the night."

"He must have exerted quite the influence because of how you live today."

"He offered an option for an alternative, simpler lifestyle. The next morning he was gone before I woke up. He left a note thanking me for my hospitality and telling me time would eventually dull the pain. He knew from experience. I kept the note. A week later, I bought my Jeep." I pointed toward my rig. "I bought what I thought would be necessary to begin *overlanding*. I was a novice, but I learned quickly. Mostly through trial and error, and I loved the solitude. I thought about returning to New England, and made it as far as New York before stopping. I wasn't ready to deal with the memories. I looked at my map. I carried paper maps. I knew I wanted to head west because it would be farthest away from New England. We had never been out west, but often talked about taking Reid on vacation there. I closed my eyes and picked a spot on the map. It was Utah. I left the next morning. I made a brief stop in SoHam..."

"Where is that?"

"It's what locals call South Hampshire."

"I see. Back in Illinois. Please continue."

"I stopped to say goodbye to my parents and pick up Bandit. I stocked up..."

"Wait!" The professor waved his hands. "Wasn't he already with you?"

"No. Bandit was with me in Michigan, but I wasn't sure I could take care of him while I was wandering around the country."

"I see now. Totally understandable."

Bandit put a paw on my knee when he heard his name.

"I decided we would share the journey. Bandit missed Reid and Noura, too. I decided to be spontaneous, take my time, and stop when I felt like it. We would drive a few hours each day, camp on the cheap as much as possible. I learned it was called boondocking. We got sidetracked and ended up in South Dakota. We meandered for a time and eventually reached Colorado. Once I got to the mountains, I was hooked. I've spent most the last two years overlanding in Colorado, Utah, Arizona." I shrugged and added, "New Mexico. Pretty much every state in the Southwest. I love being able to go from the barren desert to the high mountains."

"Do you plan to return to your former life?"

"I don't intend to wander the desert for fifty years, but I will never return to my father's law firm. I might find a place in Colorado to settle down. I could take the exam to get licensed and open a small practice. My life will never be as complicated as before."

"Life is never as simple as we would like it to be."

I paused and stared into the fire for a moment. I looked at him and said, "I was raised Catholic. Catholic school, confirmation. The whole bit. I would attend mass once a month, or more."

"What about confession?"

I shrugged. "I stopped during college. I didn't see the point anymore. I had friends who would go and make up stuff just to... I don't know... feel less guilty about their life."

"I've never belonged to an organized religion, but I've never doubted the existence of God."

"I used to believe in God, and, believe it or not, I once considered becoming a priest." I chuckled and added, "Then I learned what a vow of chastity meant."

The professor smiled but didn't speak.

"I once believed in a benevolent God, who created the universe and loved each of us, but not anymore. I refuse to believe in a God who would cause us such pain." I paused, waved my hand and repeated, "I absolutely refuse to believe."

The professor gazed into the Sage Canyon sky, winked and whispered, "You will, son, you will."

Chapter Seven

I slept restlessly in the rooftop tent that night. Bandit slept under the Jeep. I think he wanted the freedom to chase rabbits. I woke up before the sunlight entered the canyon, and started to close up the tent. I chuckled and chose to leave it set up. I took a cold shower and put on my cleanest dirty clothes. I whistled for Bandit, and he appeared a moment later.

"Did you catch another rabbit?"

His tail wagged furiously when he heard that word.

"Maybe we will find one later."

After breakfast I spent the day exploring the eastern end of the canyon. I scrambled over the boulders at the base of the cliff working my way closer to the waterfall. I hoisted myself onto one ledge after another until I was a couple hundred feet above the valley floor.

"I guess it's too late to think about it now, but I sure hope I can get down," I said to the birds nesting in a hole in the rock.

I wriggled along this ledge until I reached the waterfall. Though the storm was a distant memory to the desiccated ground, the waterfall was still being fed by the mesa above. Standing this close to the sheer wall was not the ideal way to look for the source of a spring, if one indeed existed. The professor stated this waterfall ran most of the year, so I knew there had to be an additional water source to supplement the occasional rain.

I quickly realized the futility of trying to locate the *source* and bade goodbye to the squawking birds and descended close to the same route I used to climb. Fortunately, the cracks and ledges were dry and not covered by the red dirt which dominated the valley floor. My footing was secure, and as long as I didn't look up, or straight down, my fear of heights didn't induce a sense of vertigo. I recalled the trips to the Appalachian Mountains of my youth, and how my father and grandfather insisted I learn to climb. I developed a false courage and would never confess my fear of falling.

Later, when I was scrambling over, around and under the large boulders, some of which would dwarf the Jeep, I encountered my first rattlesnake. I heard it before I saw it and froze. I spotted it a split-second before it slithered under a rock and disappeared. When I described the encounter to the professor later, he assured me the snake's bite would be painful but not necessarily fatal. He had been bitten three times over the years and now carried three different kinds of snakebite antidotes.

This day I had stashed my backpack on a flat rock in one of the cave-like depressions in the cliff. I took time to eat and drink until I was full, since I didn't plan to return to base camp until time for dinner. Bandit accompanied me as I explored this end of the canyon. From a distance the walls appeared to be smooth and give the canyon a rounded appearance. However, upon closer inspection, I found the walls to be fragmented by cracks and angles. They were anything but smooth. I noticed a desert varnish on some sections of the walls.

This I learned later from the professor was formed by clay and the iron and magnesium oxide leeching out of the porous, but stable, rock. Where this varnish existed, I looked for evidence of ancient petroglyphs and pictographs. I found a few faded examples of both. I marveled at the patience of the natives to carve the petroglyphs into the walls. In the few places I saw pictographs, I wondered how they made their *ink* or *paint*, and how it had lasted so long. I assumed the dry desert air enabled their art to survive for hundreds of years.

I found what I assumed to be the ruins of an ancient Indian dwelling. Many of the foundation stones were still in place, and, in a few places, I found the flat stones of what must have been the walls. I peered closely and was impressed by the craftsmanship. There was a flat, round rock in the middle. I sat and pondered how the uncomplicated life of these ancient natives compared to today's technology dependent society. I closed my eyes and allowed my imagination to drift. I chuckled remembering the Westerns my grandfather watched religiously. Only the scenery in those productions had any resemblance to reality. For an eerie moment I sensed the spirit of the people who had lived in the valley in the distant past. When I heard a chilling wind, and saw little dust devils, I jumped up and left. The professor informed me later this was probably a grinding stone and most likely also used to make sacrifices to their ancestors and gods. His wry smile caused doubt in my mind about the sacrifices, but the eerie sensation was completely real.

I discovered another ruin on a shelf above me. I scrambled up, peered inside the much smaller ruin and saw what I thought to be several corn cobs covered by a spiderweb in the far corner. I knew enough about cliff dwellings to realize this must have been a granary. I gazed at the valley floor and pictured the inhabitants working in their gardens. Sage Canyon must have supported a large Indian population at one time. There was fertile ground, an abundant supply of fresh water and the canyon walls provided security. Other than rock slides, I assumed the canyon walls hadn't changed much in the last millennium.

After making my way down from the ledge, I spent the rest of the afternoon exploring the valley floor. I tried to identify the different flora, but some plants were completely foreign to me. I thought about the Indian medicine men and how they knew which plants to use to cure common illnesses. I lamented the loss of this knowledge in modern medicine.

I stumbled upon two other foundations and explored them to pass away the time. I recalled the professor's story about a hidden treasure. I didn't want to believe his story, but it could be true. I used a stick to poke around the ruins but stopped after a time.

I laughed and told Bandit, "If Zenus Sage did hide a treasure, it wouldn't be in the Indian ruins."

He ignored me and barked at an annoying bird.

I watched small lizards scurrying through the dirt and pictured an age when dinosaurs possibly roamed the canyon, or more likely the mesa top.

By the time I returned to camp, the sun illuminated only the uppermost sections of the canyon walls. I marveled at the different colors created by light and shadows. The professor had prepared another simple meal, and he asked questions about the day's explorations. I mentioned the ruins, and this was when he smiled and told me about the sacrifices.

I slept in my rooftop tent again that night and lay awake for hours listening to the wind raising voices from the dust.

Chapter Eight

↗

I spent the next four days exploring the canyon from one end to the other. Bandit would keep me company, and each afternoon he would disappear for a time and later return with something for dinner.

One day he returned with an animal I had never seen before. It was a squirrel of some sort, but nothing like the ones from home. The professor told me it was a common canyon squirrel unique to the area. Over the ages it had adapted to its environment developing large ears and a reddish gray color, which was the perfect camouflage.

"Who in the valley, other than Bandit, might prey on the squirrels?"

The professor pointed up. "Eagles and hawks."

"Bandit is too large for them to carry off, right?"

He nodded.

"No pterodactyls in the area, right?" I asked facetiously.

He stared upward for ten seconds at least, turned his eyes toward me and whispered solemnly, "I haven't seen one all summer." He raised a hand and added, "But it's still early."

I stared at him for an eternity and a half. His expression never changed from that of a man concerned for his well-being as his eyes darted from one section of sky to another.

A short time later we listened to a noise unlike any I had ever heard. He jumped to his feet, pointed skyward then covered his head with both hands. I heard the noise again. It sounded like a cross between a truck's air horn and the bleating of a mountain goat. I couldn't see the creature responsible for the sound, but I saw a large shadow fly overhead.

I stared at the professor after the noise abated. "What was that? Tell me it wasn't a..."

Only then did his expression change. Slowly a smile spread over his leathery face. He pointed at me and said, "Gotcha!"

"Wait! I heard it, and I saw its shadow. That wasn't an eagle or hawk."

He laughed so hard, and for so long, that *my* sides began to hurt.

"Are you finished amusing yourself at my expense?"

"I'm sorry. I couldn't resist."

"What was it?"

"Simply a desert turkey vulture with an injured voice box."

"How do you know?"

"I hit it with a rock when it was trying to steal my supper a few summers back."

"The shadow was massive."

He shook his head. "It's a trick of the sun. The light, and shadows, play tricks with your mind. It is a large bird, but not a threat to Bandit," he said, paused and added, "Or to either of us."

I cooked supper that evening. Since Bandit hadn't provided any fresh meat, I used one of the packaged meals I had purchased from REI. This one was called Three Sisters Stew.

"Smells pretty good," the professor said looking over my shoulder as I used my Coleman stove. "What's in it?"

I read directly from the package, "The Native American holy trinity of corn, beans, and squash becomes a tasty, hearty, high-protein stew with brown rice and quinoa."

"It might be better with some rabbit or venison."

"I'll try that next time."

He checked out the shelf on the tailgate of my Jeep. "Pretty fancy get-up. Was it expensive?"

"Depends," I replied.

"A thimble of water would be a torrential flood to a man dying of thirst."

I stared at the professor.

He shrugged and said, "One of my students once wrote that on a test. It humored me, so I use it occasionally."

I pointed to the folding table. "Amazon. Less than $150, and I consider it a bargain."

We sat in my camp chairs to eat without any more conversation.

"Not bad for something out of a bag," he said after scraping his plate clean.

"There's a little left. Would you like it?"

"Don't mind if I do."

"I was never much of a cook, so I bought a bunch of meals in a bag when I started my journey. I have a few left, but I've taught myself how to cook a decent meal."

"Necessity is the mother of invention."

"Another student?"

"Frank Zappa fan."

Cleaning up took me ten minutes. He started a fire, though the evening was still warm.

"What did you learn the last few days?" He pulled a battered pipe from his flannel shirt and clenched it in his jaw.

"I thought you gave up smoking years ago?"

"I gave up tobacco. Not my pipe."

It was the first time I had seen him with his *old pipe*.

"Old habits, huh?"

"It helps me think. Like Sherlock Holmes."

I watched the fire for a moment. The flames rose into the air with a sizzle and then disappeared without a trace, but I could still feel the effects.

"I didn't find the treasure, but I didn't focus everything on the search."

He raised his bushy eyebrows.

We sat without the need to hear the sound of our voices. The only sounds were the campfire, the barely discernible babbling of the creek and the ever-present harmonies of various wildlife. No injured turkey vulture interrupted our reverie.

After several minutes, I said, "I might have found a way out."

Again, his eyebrows moved. His pipe moved in rhythm with his eyebrows as he spoke out of the side of his mouth, "Where?"

I stood and pointed to the north wall. "Two miles, give or take. Just past a rockslide. I was able to climb about three hundred feet."

"That still leaves several hundred feet to go," he said with a wry smile.

"We have tools, and strong backs..."

"Speak for yourself."

"I could work on a trail."

He sighed, closed his eyes and chewed on his pipe for a time.

"I don't want to live here forever."

He opened his eyes and asked, "Do you have somewhere you need to be?"

"Not really, but I thought I would be in California by the fall. I might be stuck in Sage Canyon for decades."

"Not a bad place to be stranded."

I remembered he had been exploring the canyon for most of his life.

The fire died down, and he decided to retire early.

"I would like to see the vehicle you mentioned soon."

He chuckled and asked, "Are you busy tomorrow? Do you need to check your appointment book?"

"I have briefs and motions to write in the morning, but might have the afternoon free."

"Be ready to do some scrambling." He waved and left me alone with my thoughts. And Bandit.

Later, I was close to falling asleep when I sat up suddenly. A distant, faint sound had disturbed my ears. I climbed down, stood beside the Jeep and listened. The remote sound echoed off the walls. Bandit rubbed against my leg. His tail was not wagging. I stared at the stars and the full moon.

"Bandit, either this canyon is playing tricks on my mind, or those are drums I'm hearing." I put a hand to my ear. "And I'm not talking about a drum solo by Dave Persching. It sounds like... like..."

I heard a whizzing sound then something striking metal. I looked around, and there was enough moonlight for me to see an arrow next to the Jeep.

Chapter Nine

↗

"Bandit! Come with me!"

I fell to my knees as I slipped in the red dirt while scurrying around the Jeep. Bandit crawled under it. My heart pounded double time. I sat with my back against the driver's side rear tire. I listened for the drums, but couldn't hear anything. I didn't stir for five minutes before finally gaining enough courage to move. I stood and quickly peeked over the hood. I could see nothing but the black canvas of the canyon walls with millions of stars overhead and the moon. I ducked down and waited several more minutes before standing up straight. Bandit crawled out and sat beside me.

"Can you hear anything? I can't."

Bandit cocked his head and beat his tail against the tire.

"That's not helping," I said then chuckled.

For a moment, I wondered if it had all been a dream. A nightmare brought on by the memories of the Westerns my grandfather watched. I duckwalked around the Jeep while swiveling my head from one canyon wall to another. I paused by the passenger-side front fender and didn't see anything at first. I looked a second time. It hadn't been a dream. On the ground three feet from the Jeep was an arrow. A broken arrow.

"Bandit, it wasn't a dream."

He barked at the arrow, but then backed away.

I made myself as small a target as possible as I moved around the Jeep. No more arrows whizzed through the night air. I picked up the two pieces of the wooden arrow. I assumed it had been broken by the contact with the Jeep.

"Why would anyone fire a single arrow at us, Bandit? Is someone trying to frighten me into leaving the canyon? Are they protecting the treasure?"

Bandit didn't answer. He crawled under the Jeep and rolled in the dirt.

"Is there an undercover army protecting the secrets of Sage Canyon?" I thought about stories of ancient Egyptian mummies and undiscovered tombs holding riches beyond belief and chuckled. "Only in the movies."

I climbed back into the tent and slept fitfully until morning.

I emerged cautiously from the tent. Bandit was sleeping at the bottom of the ladder. *Good boy, Bandit. You were protecting me.* He woke up when I started climbing down. He stretched out and wagged his tail to greet me.

"Good job, Bandit. You defended us from further attack."

I put on my boots, picked up both pieces of the broken arrow, and did a quick search of the immediate area. No more arrows. I knew the professor was up because I could smell his special brew of coffee. I took care of urgent business and headed up the canyon to show him the arrow.

"Coffee's ready. Help yourself," he said while mixing the flour to make biscuits.

"Thanks, Professor." I poured a cup. "I need to show you something."

He turned around, saw what I was holding and laughed.

"This almost killed me last night. It's not a laughing matter."

"That arrow might have bruised you, but it's not lethal." He took part of the arrow. "Now if this *arrowhead* was sharp, it would be dangerous. This wouldn't penetrate one of my fresh biscuits." He handed it back.

I inspected the tip again. It was pear-shaped with the fatter part on the end and made of a soft rubber.

"Who would shoot this at me? And why?"

"Chief Joseph Paledeer."

"Who is that?"

"In his words he is a descendant of the last chief of the Southern Utes. Ol' Joe is harmless. He lives down in Bluff, and once, or twice, a year, he goes on a rampage. Usually preceded by a visit to the Broken Bottle Saloon. His oldest son pulls the horse trailer up here, and Ol' Joe rides his horse to the top of Piqua Mesa."

"Why?"

The professor shrugged. "He calls it a spiritual journey."

"What about the attack?" I asked looking at the arrow again. He might have sent me on a *spiritual journey*."

The professor shook his head. "He fires these arrows at my campsite. Most years he will ride into the canyon and spend a few days with me."

"This is serious. It's a matter for the authorities. He attacked me last night. This arrow hit the Jeep while I was standing next to it."

"Coincidence."

"I don't think so," I replied trying not to let my anger rise.

"I assure you Ol' Joe was not aiming at you, or the Jeep. He is so nearsighted it's a wonder he doesn't ride his horse off the edge of a mesa somewhere. He's too vain to wear his glasses unless he's driving. He tries to aim at where he thinks I might be, but he couldn't hit the canyon wall with a missile." The professor walked outside, shielded his eyes and peered up at the mesa. "I hope he doesn't attempt to descend the old trail. He wouldn't see the area destroyed by the avalanche."

I followed and asked, "Would his horse?"

"Probably. We will know soon. We'll either find his body at the bottom of the cliff, or he will ride around to the slot canyon."

"He knows where to find it?"

The professor laughed. "Not Ol' Joe. Flies Over Clouds. His horse."

I raised my eyebrows. "The horse knows how to find the slot canyon?"

"Yes. He will lead Joe as close as he can then Joe will eventually feel the wind from the slot and squeeze through."

"Okay, I have to ask. Why did he name his horse Flies Over Clouds? I assume that's the English translation of some Indian name."

"Joe claims it is. Truth be known, he doesn't speak any more Ute than you or I. If he does make it into the canyon, he will try to impress you."

"How?"

"He will..." The professor pointed. "Here he comes. I will let him explain."

I watched as a tall, white-haired man with skin as brown and tough-looking as slickrock approached. He was wearing jeans tucked into boots made from the hide of some animal.

"Hello, my old friend!" the professor hollered. He turned to me and whispered, "I yell so he knows where I am. He can be rather prideful."

I watched as Chief Joseph slowly made his way toward us.

"It's good to see you, Joe." The professor made his way to his old friend and they exchanged hugs.

"I am happy to see you, Talks Too Much," Ol' Joe said.

I glanced at the professor and mouthed the same words.

"I'll explain later," the professor whispered. "I have a friend with me, Chief. His name is Rhett Carter. He's one of those high-powered lawyers from the big city who decided to take time away from charging clients a fortune and learn how the rest of the world lives."

I shook my head and scowled at the professor.

The professor waved me closer, and I walked up and shook hands with the old Indian.

He straightened up and raised a hand high into the air. I thought he might say 'How' like the pitifully portrayed Indians in early westerns. In my peripheral vision I saw the professor with a hand to his mouth stifling a laugh.

Instead, he stood as straight as a totem pole and said proudly in perfect English, "I am Chief Joseph Paledeer. The last of my tribe to preserve our way of life. I have come to reclaim my ancestral land which was stolen from my people by the white man many years ago. I have not surrendered, and will fight until the last drop of my blood soaks into the red dirt of Sage Canyon."

I looked at the professor.

"I respect your quest to resurrect the honor of your people," the professor said. "Rhett is on a quest of his own."

Chief Joseph turned to me and nodded, acknowledging our shared goals.

"Now, how about some coffee and breakfast?" the professor asked. "I'm starving."

"I accept your hospitality. It took me all night to ride to the slot canyon. Flies Over Clouds refused to take the trail down Piqua Mesa."

The professor told him about the rockslide.

"I owe my life to Flies Over Clouds," Chief Joseph said solemnly.

"Where is your horse?" I asked because I didn't see it anywhere.

"He will be waiting at the slot canyon when I return."

"In your dreams, Ol' Joe. Your son followed in the truck and will take Flies Over Clouds home. You'll make me take you home when I decide to leave."

Ol' Joe looked in my direction. "It wasn't always like this. I could see better than an eagle as a young warrior. Now I rely on others to get around."

We sat in the cave to eat.

"Joe worked at the university with me until I retired," the professor said. "Occasionally, he would sit in on one of my lectures."

I smiled and added, "Thus the name."

"I suspect lawyers have the same fault."

I turned to Joe and asked, "What were the lectures like? Did you enjoy them?"

Joe chewed deliberately, took a swig of coffee, stared at the professor for a moment then turned to me. "The lectures contained much information about a subject the professor is passionate about." He drained his coffee cup quickly and added, "They were also as interesting as watching cryptobiotic soil grow."

I laughed and said, "Two years ago I wouldn't have understood your reference, but after spending time in the desert, I get it."

"My lectures were instructional and intended to teach my students," the professor said in his defense.

"Yes, if they understood your terminology," Joe replied.

"They understood me."

Joe looked at me and shook his head.

I chuckled. "My father would use fifty, multisyllable words when two or three simple words would have made his point. Some people thought he was a great orator, I think it was a case of him enjoying the sound of his own voice."

"Joe, I hate to mention it, but one of your arrows hit Rhett's Jeep last night. You frightened him. He thought he was under attack."

Ol' Joe looked in my direction. "Is this true? I wounded your Jeep?"

"Wounded might be too strong, but you definitely hit it and there's a small scratch."

"I am sorry for the destruction of your vehicle, but I am on a quest for my people. It is most unfortunate there will be collateral damage."

I was speechless for a moment.

Then the professor and Ol' Joe lost it. They high-fived each other and laughed until they fell off the rocks they were sitting on.

"I don't understand."

Bandit watched the two men and tilted his head back and forth as he sat beside me.

Eventually, they stopped laughing and sat on their rocks again.

"I apologize, Rhett," the professor said. "Thirty years ago I made a bet with Joe that he would never hit anything but the canyon floor with his arrows. He claimed his accuracy was guided by his ancestors and did not need the use of his physical eyes."

"Last night the spirits of my ancestors guided my arrow to what I thought was a blue buffalo. I thought it was a symbol of the white man and by killing it, I would avenge my people."

I stared at Joe, then the professor. The professor was grinning. I turned back to Joe and listened.

Ol' Joe sighed, raised his face and hands to the sky and said, "I know now my ancestors' spirits are as blind as me."

Chapter Ten

ʌ

I shook my head. "I really thought my life was in danger."

"It's a miracle his arrow hit your Jeep," the professor said.

I looked at Ol' Joe for a moment then snapped my fingers. "Wait a minute. What about the drums I heard? How do you explain that?"

"My people have always used drums to summon the spirits before we enter into battle with our enemies. No matter what color or creed," Ol' Joe said sincerely.

The professor chortled.

Joe sighed and pulled a cell phone from a pocket. "All right. I use this and a Bluetooth speaker to let Talks Too Much know I am here. I almost gave him a heart attack years ago by tapping him on the shoulder. He didn't know I was behind him. I vowed to never sneak up on him again."

The professor waved both hands emphatically. "He hasn't been able to sneak up on me for twenty years. Don't believe his tripe."

The old Indian stared in my direction. "Why are you in the canyon? Are you a treasure seeker hoping to find what many before have failed to discover? Do you have a map marked with an X?" He sighed and lowered his head. "I had a vision of thousands of white men invading the canyon. Is this the start?"

I shook my head then remembered he couldn't see clearly. "No, Chief Joseph. I knew nothing about the treasure until the professor told me that fanciful tale a few days ago."

"Did you get lost?" he asked. "No one searches out this canyon intentionally. A few locals know of its existence, but it is not a tourist destination."

"As the professor mentioned, I am on a quest myself. I'm searching for a new direction in my life."

"And a wrong turn in your journey brought you to Sage Canyon, right?"

I told him about my overlanding adventures. The professor added the part about losing my family.

"I am sorry for your sorrow," Joe said. "White men have many strange customs my people do not understand, but this quest to find peace after your great loss, I understand."

"Let me ask you this, Joe. Do you believe in the legend of Zenus Gage and his so-called treasure?"

"I believe many legends are based on partial truths."

I crossed my arms over my chest.

The professor chuckled and said, "He doesn't buy your BS, Joe. I think he wants a straight answer. He's a lawyer from the Midwest. No sense of humor."

"Am I under oath? My people have always spoken the truth even though the white man deceived us over the years."

The professor rolled his eyes and muttered, "Cut the crap, Joe."

"No, you are not under oath, but the professor is right. I would like a straight answer."

Ol' Joe turned on his rock to face me. "I believe Zenus Gage found something here. Gold? Silver?" He shrugged. "It's possible. But this I truly believe. I believe Zenus died in this canyon, and it wasn't from old age. Many times I have been exploring the canyon and felt as if someone was watching me." He waved a hand. "It's as though the spirit of those who have searched in vain, and lost their lives in the process, are still here waiting for someone to discover Zenus Gage's mysterious treasure. Maybe they are protecting it."

"I know this sounds crazy, but I've felt the same thing." I explained the circumstances and the feeling in my gut of being observed stealthily.

"Maybe it was a drone," the professor said with a shrug.

"I know the difference. Definitely not a drone."

"The people who know about the treasure are few now, but they are becoming more desperate," Joe said. "I've seen evidence of them on the mesa."

The professor laughed. "Without your glasses, you can't see any farther than three feet away."

I spent the rest of the morning going through the Jeep. I sorted through my clothes and inventoried my food supply. Not sure why because I obviously couldn't run into town and go shopping. I thought about using the satellite phone to call my father to let him know my location and circumstances.

"Bandit, if I make the call, my father will do everything in his power to force me back home. Do we really want to end our adventure early?"

Bandit listened, but didn't answer.

I put the phone away.

After lunch the professor asked, "Are you ready to search for the vehicle I mentioned? I haven't seen it in years, but I think I can find it again. I know the general area."

"Is it worth the effort to find it?"

He chuckled and answered, "That would be up to you."

"I don't have any appointments on the calendar," I said as a joke. "Let's do it."

"Joe, do you want to tag along?"

"You need my expert tracking skills. Without me you could search for weeks and never find it."

The professor whispered, "What he means is he might get lost if we leave him here alone."

"I heard that," Ol' Joe said. "When one sense is weak, the others are strengthened."

The professor elbowed my ribs and whispered, "He's going deaf, too."

Since the sun was partly obscured by clouds that appeared to be hammered into place, and the temperature was in the upper 70s, we decided not to drive the Jeep.

"How much farther?" I asked listening for Bandit, who had decided to hunt for his dinner. "We've been hiking over two hours.

The professor studied the north wall of the canyon. After scrutinizing it for nearly a minute, he pointed. "Do you see that round boulder wedged into the crack about a hundred feet below the rim?"

I unzipped my backpack, took out my binoculars, turned my cap around and tried to find the boulder. I scanned the area he described and eventually spotted it. "Is that where it is?"

"If I remember correctly, the vehicle should be a quarter mile west. Give or take."

The way he said *vehicle* made me think it wasn't an ordinary car or truck.

We made our way closer to the north wall. The vegetation was thicker along here because the creek was only a hundred feet from the base of the wall. Surprisingly, the wall came straight down to the valley floor. There was no debris from previous rockslides to climb. There were boulders to negotiate, but nothing too technical. We hiked for thirty minutes before the professor stopped.

"Are we close?" I asked.

"We should be, but I don't see it." He looked behind us in case we had overshot it. "Things have changed since the last time I was here."

I climbed on top of a boulder to see over the chest-high vegetation and said, "It might help if I knew exactly what we were searching for."

Ol' Joe was about to tell me when the professor hollered, "I see it! We must have walked within ten feet of it without spotting the blasted thing."

71

The professor led the way and we were soon staring at the remains of a hot air balloon. The wicker basket was semi-intact, but the canopy, which was silk fabric, had deteriorated considerably. Vegetation grew through everything. Of the ropes which must have secured the canopy to the basket, there was no evidence.

"I was expecting a more modern vehicle."

The professor laughed.

"Where are the burners?"

"I assume they were metal and taken away to be used elsewhere."

"How old is this? How long has it been here?"

"I did some research, and this might date from just after the Civil War," he answered. "As to your second question, I have no idea. I discovered it thirty years ago."

"Did you find the pilot?"

He shook his head. "I have always assumed he died in the canyon, possibly from injuries sustained in the crash, and what remained of his bones was scattered by the wildlife that once roamed here. I certainly didn't find his skull."

I examined the basket closer. One side appeared to have been damaged and a crash would be the most likely cause.

"The dry air must have helped preserve it. Did you ever find anything from the basket? Something that might have weighed it down."

"I know you're asking about gold and silver. I did not find anything, but that doesn't mean earlier explorers to the valley didn't find something."

I walked all the way around the basket searching for evidence.

"What are you looking for?" the professor asked. "You won't find anything of value."

"I didn't expect to see gold bars stacked in neat rows waiting to be hauled away," I replied. "Could the brothers you told me about earlier have known this was here?"

The professor scratched his ear. "My guess would be no. Personally, I believe this balloon crashed here in the 1880s, but I have no scientific evidence to support my theory."

Ol' Joe got close enough to see the wicker basket, shrugged and asked what should have been an obvious question. "Did this crash while landing in the canyon, or did it crash attempting to leave?"

I looked at the professor for the answer.

He tugged on his beard, shrugged and replied, "I don't suppose there's any way to tell at this point. The basket was empty when I found it, and the canopy was pretty much as you see it now."

"I don't know how quickly silk deteriorates, but it is a natural material," I said. "The ropes have totally disappeared."

The professor broke off a piece of the wicker. "I don't know much about hot air balloons, but I think if whoever was using this one was carrying gold or any other heavy minerals, they would have needed a stronger basket and a much larger balloon. It's a long way to the rim."

"They could have made several trips."

"This is true," Joe said as he attempted move a tree branch that had fallen on the canopy.

"What are you doing?" the professor asked.

"There might be something of value under the canopy."

I heard a now somewhat familiar sound and gazed up at the rim barely in time to holler, "Look out!" I pushed the professor and Joe out of the way as a boulder somehow became dislodged and landed twenty feet from where we were standing.

Chapter Eleven

ↄ

"That was mighty close," the professor said as I helped him to his feet.

We looked up but didn't see anyone, or anymore rocks heading our way.

"I don't think this crashed where it did accidentally," I said. "I think someone loosened it and relied on gravity to do the damage."

"It would be quite a coincidence if it happened naturally."

We both turned around when we heard Ol' Joe moaning. He was sitting up by now with a hand to the back of his head.

"Are you okay?"

He rubbed the back of his head and when he moved his hand, I could see blood. We helped him to his feet, and I inspected the wound.

"Is it my time?" Joe asked. "Should I do my death dance now?"

"Do you know one?" the professor asked.

He rubbed the back of his head again and said, "I could fake it."

The professor turned his back to Joe.

"There's no need. It's a small scratch. You must have hit your head when I pushed you."

"I am ready to join my ancestors. Tell me the truth for once, white man."

The professor pulled a red bandana from his back pocket, and wrapped it around Joe's head. "I'll send you on your way if you don't stop acting like your ancestors. This isn't the 1880s. Chances are you will outlive all of us."

Ol' Joe stood up straight. He backed away from the cliff, used a hand to shield the sun and stared at the rim. "That's strange."

"Do you see anything?" I asked.

"Didn't there used to be a canyon wall nearby? All I see is a blur."

That blur suddenly came into focus as three more boulders bounced off the wall. In less than five seconds these boulders landed with a thud that shook the ground. Expecting more boulders to fall, we dashed toward the wall and dove into a small opening below an outcrop of rock.

"We should be safe here, but if the whole wall decides to collapse, no one will ever find our bodies."

The professor pointed to the boulders. "They didn't fall because of an avalanche, or natural erosion. Had that been the case, we would already be covered by tons of rock and debris."

"And I would have joined my ancestors for real," Joe added.

"Individual boulders occasionally fall, but four in the space of a couple minutes is not a coincidence. Someone did this intentionally."

"I will avenge our honor," Joe swore.

"They were trying to kill us?" I asked.

"Perhaps. But I suspect they were trying to scare us out of the canyon. Had they wanted to murder us, they would have used rifles."

We waited in our position of relative safety for ten minutes.

"I think it's safe to come out," the professor said.

"You go first." Joe pointed at me. "I'll stay here in case the professor is wrong."

"Joe, you are the most cowardly Indian I've ever met."

"Courage is overrated. I value patience in these situations."

I emerged cautiously and crept along the wall for a distance before standing up and looking at the rim. No more boulders fell. We did not hear the muted sound of a rifle. I could not see anyone standing at the edge of the cliff.

"I think it's safe now."

The professor appeared first then Joe materialized a moment later.

""I wish I had my bow with me," Joe said. "I would dissuade those recreant hooligans from further attempts on our lives."

The professor sighed. I chuckled. Joe smiled.

We didn't stick around in case more boulders became conveniently dislodged. Bandit joined us a moment later carrying one of the canyon squirrels softly in his mouth. He dropped it at my feet.

"Good job, Bandit. Can you carry it to camp?"

He grabbed his dinner and scampered off in the direction of the Jeep.

"How much effort have you put into searching for the treasure," I asked the professor as we headed back up the trail.

"Not much in recent years. Twenty years ago Joe and I spent an entire summer searching."

"I could see better then," Joe reminded me.

"Mines leave a trace. You can find evidence without much effort. We wasted three months exploring the canyon for even a small remnant of a mine without success."

"If Sage mined the canyon in the 1820s, or earlier, is it possible nature has reclaimed the site?" I asked.

The professor pointed to the vegetation near the creek. "If the mine was in the valley, I would say it's possible. Highly likely, in fact. No one can say with any certainty if Sage's treasure was mined out of the rock, or if he found it panning in the creek." He pointed to the north wall. "Most mines are found in the rock. In this case, the canyon walls. We mapped the walls with diligence and made note of anything looking like a possible site. We inspected over a hundred possibilities without finding anything other than Indian artifacts."

"Which you stole from my people to place in your museum," Joe said with a frown. He crossed his arms over his chest and stood still as we walked away.

When his comment didn't evoke a response, he hollered, "Hey! Wait for me. I could get lost and wander around for years."

"We could only hope for such a gift," the professor said.

"Since you didn't find the mine, have you discounted the legend?"

The professor stopped. I took a few more steps before realizing he was no longer beside me.

"Is it merely a myth? A tall tale told by Zenus Sage all those years ago?"

"I would have ignored the stories years ago except for this." He reached into his pocket and pulled something out. He opened his hand and let the marble-sized object rest in his palm.

"Is that?"

"Yes," he nodded.

I had never seen such a large amount of gold before, but I could tell this nugget would be worth spending the time and resources to find the legendary Zenus Sage mine.

"How long have you had that?" I asked though I desperately wanted to ask *where* he found it.

The professor snapped his hand closed and pocketed the nugget. "I found it two weeks ago."

I removed my cap, slapped it against my thigh several times as I pondered the implications for a moment.

Joe caught up to us and asked, "What are we going to do about the boulders? Someone, or several people are watching us. I can feel it in my bones." He waved a hand at the professor. "It's not my arthritis. I can tell the difference."

"We need to be vigilant, and stay away from the canyon walls," I suggested.

"That will work in avoiding boulders, but what if our enemy begins using firearms?" Joe asked.

"Then we... I have no idea. I've never been shot at," I said with a shrug. "With a rifle, I mean. I was attacked with arrows."

"It was one arrow, and I was shooting at the blue buffalo," Joe said defensively.

"I agree with the need to be vigilant, but we cannot avoid searching close to the walls." The professor stopped and stared at the debris along the south canyon wall. He slapped his forehead and muttered, "How could I have been so stupid?"

Chapter Twelve

"What are you talking about?" I asked the professor.

He pointed to the debris at the bottom of the south wall and whispered, "It has to be there."

I cocked my head to the right and heard my neck pop. "That exact spot? How can you be so positive? Those rocks look the same as all the others along the base of the cliff."

He ignored my question for a moment.

Joe joined us and stared at the professor. He then told me, "I've seen this before. He is thinking."

"Yeah, I kinda gathered that."

Then the professor snapped out of his trance and smiled. I repeated my question.

He shook his head and waved his hands. "Not that exact spot, but if you wanted to hide a cactus, where would you hide it?"

"What type of cactus?" Joe asked. "Not all cacti live in the same regions."

"Doesn't matter," the professor said. "Don't over complicate the question."

"In a desert," I answered with a shrug.

"Exactly!" He clapped his hands together, and, for a brief second, I thought he was going to dance a jig. His feet began to move in time to a rhythm only understood, or heard, by him.

I stared at the professor and whispered to Joe, "I take it this is a good sign, right?"

"Either that, or when he fell earlier, he sustained a concussion and he's lost his mind. I've also seen evidence of that in the past."

The professor stopped dancing, snapped his fingers, and said, "We must hurry! We have no time to waste. I know exactly where to find the treasure." He turned and began walking toward camp with a renewed vigor. "I've been a fool for forty years. It's been so obvious this entire time."

I looked at Joe again. He moved a finger around his ear indicating madness.

"Hey, Professor!" I hollered hurrying to catch up to him. "Would you mind telling us what's been so obvious?"

He walked faster than I had ever witnessed, determined to make it back as quickly as possible.

"Zenus Gage, you were mad after all," the professor hollered and his voice echoed off the canyon walls. "You were a mad genius."

The professor trudged into camp three hours after sunset looking more depressed than someone who had just lost their favorite dog. He sat on one of the boulders, slumped his shoulders and shook his head.

"Not where you thought, huh?" I asked handing him a mug of coffee. "Sorry for asking the question when the answer is so obvious. There's food left from supper if you're hungry."

"It's got to be there," he said then took a sip of the hot brew. "It's the only place that makes sense." He took another sip and stared into the campfire. "People have scoured every inch of this canyon, so it has to be there."

I fixed him a plate of beans and potatoes, set it next to him and said, "You always find something in the last place you look."

"Unless you never find it."

He finished his first plate and handed it to me.

"More?"

He nodded.

I fixed him a second plate.

"Thanks," he said while staring into space.

"Are you going to tell me where you were searching?"

"I'll show you tomorrow. I'm too exhausted and disappointed to go back tonight."

After breakfast, Joe and I followed the professor to the waterfall. I could see evidence of the previous day's work. There were overturned boulders and piles of disturbed red dirt in numerous places.

"Why did you think this was the place?" I picked up one of the smaller boulders, turned it over and saw a small crystal embedded in it.

"This is the only area of the canyon I haven't searched thoroughly over the years."

"Why haven't you looked here?"

Bandit scrambled over, under, around and through the debris field in search of a meal.

"The waterfall may be a trickle now, but forty years ago it was ten times this size. There was no way to search this area. That's why I thought the ore would be here."

"It might still be here," I said checking the fresh piles of dirt.

He shook his head. "If the treasure was as large as legend claims, there would be some indication. I found no evidence of ore, or the mine."

"Are you going to give up the quest?"

"Never!" he shouted. "I believe the treasure was real, and it still exists somewhere in Sage Canyon. It may not be my main focus, but I will keep searching as long as I'm physically able."

Joe added, "Sometimes the search is its own reward."

"Don't go getting all philosophical on me," the professor frowned.

"It's the journey that matters not the destination," I added with a shrug.

The professor and Joe moaned.

"There must be a written history of the men who discovered the canyon. There might be a clue as to the location of the treasure."

"I should have mentioned this before, but I've got a journal written by the son of one of the Hough brothers back at camp. I'll let you read it if you're interested."

I gazed in the direction of the opposite end of the canyon. "Apparently, I have all the time in the world and reading material is scarce."

"That was the last of the bread," I said after lunch. "I have a box of Saltines, and we have peanut butter."

"We won't starve as long as Bandit is around to provide us with small game," the professor said rubbing Bandit's ears.

"I'm partial to chunky peanut butter," Ol' Joe said. "But Native Americans have limited choices."

The professor headed up the slope and disappeared into his cave. He returned after a few minutes with a leather-bound book.

"Is that the journal?"

"Yes. At least what's left. Pages were removed at some point."

"The missing pages might have provided clues," I said.

The professor and Ol' Joe rolled their eyes.

"Sorry, I should have known you already knew that."

"It's not real long, but some of the pages are slightly smudged. I had one of my students make a copy, but there's still the matter of the missing pages. I gave up all hope of finding them years ago."

"Do you mind if I read this tonight?"

The professor shrugged. "Go ahead. Let me know if you need help. I've read it so many times, I've memorized whole sections."

Ol' Joe stood and pointed to the west. "My bones tell me to take cover."

"Is there another afternoon storm heading our way?"

The sky was suddenly filled with heat lightning, and I could smell the ozone.

"Unless it changes course, it could come right down the middle of the canyon," the professor answered.

We took shelter in the cave ten minutes later and sat out the storm. Bandit raced out as soon as the rain and hail stopped. I followed him to the Jeep. I wiped away the hail from the hood and shook my head.

"Bandit, I've never seen hailstones this size before." I scooped up several of the baseball-sized hailstones and tossed them toward the creek. "They've dented the hood and cracked the windshield, but the storm hasn't killed it."

Ol' Joe walked up behind me and heard my conversation with Bandit.

"The gods must be angry at your Jeep for invading this sacred canyon. Maybe my ancestors were right when they guided my arrow to its side." He turned and looked up at the top of the waterfall. "We should head to higher ground. This area will soon be flooded. If your Jeep is still alive, you might want to move it away from the creek."

The Jeep started on the second try. I put it into 4Low and drove as high up the slope as I could get. Less than a minute later we watched as the area by the creek was engulfed in a flash flood. I watched my camp chairs and cassette toilet float away.

Chapter Thirteen

↗

Two hours later the creek was only a couple feet higher than normal. I found the camp chairs lodged between a couple boulders about half a mile downstream. The plastic toilet was smashed to pieces.

"Does that happen often?" I asked the professor.

"Flash floods are common, but that was one of the worst I've experienced."

"What about the slot canyon? Will it be flooded?"

"Parts of it are always underwater. Didn't I mention swimming parts of it before?"

I shook my head. "I don't remember you mentioning it. What would it be like now?"

He smoothed out his beard as he thought. "I wouldn't want to be caught in it now. It drops a couple hundred feet in elevation. Parts would be rather deep and there would be a strong current. You could get pulled under, or smashed into a rock." He shook his hand. "Best to wait for dry weather."

I was surprised when Ol' Joe volunteered to cook dinner that evening. Then I noticed Bandit had supplied him with a freshly killed rabbit. He skinned the rabbit then disappeared down the trail for an hour. He chased us out of the cave when he returned.

"What are you hiding?" I pointed to the canvas bag he was holding.

He set the bag on the large boulder we used as a table. "I add secret ingredients to my stew."

"What exactly?"

He shook his head. "There are plants in the canyon that only my people know how to find. Some are used to cure certain ailments, others add flavor to our sustenance." He paused, grinned and added, "Some are smoked in spiritual ceremonies."

The professor chuckled and walked away. "He grows loco weed down the canyon and pretends it's for native ceremonies. Sometimes it knocks him out. Other times he hallucinates and claims to see his ancestors, the spirits of long departed creatures and demons and other frightening images. Don't inhale any of the smoke. It will knock you out for days."

I stared at Joe. "What are you going to add to the stew tonight?"

"Some herbs to give it flavor. Talks Too Much doesn't know how to cook anything. His food is always bland and tasteless. Don't worry. I won't poison you, or send you on a spiritual trip."

"Don't add too many hot peppers," the professor suggested, though it sounded like an order to me. "Rhett might not be used to spicy food."

"I enjoy spicy chili," I said in my defense. "I order hot peppers on my Darby's hot dogs."

"Maybe so," the professor said, "but some of his peppers are hot enough to melt the walls of this canyon."

"If only that were true," I sighed. "I could drive out of here tomorrow."

"Add more salt if it's too hot," Joe said later.

"It's not too hot."

By the third bite of the spiced-up rabbit stew, my eyes were watering uncontrollably. My nose and throat felt like they were being subjected to direct rays of the sun.

"Are you trying to kill him?" the professor asked taking my bowl of stew from me and tasting it himself.

"I made a separate pot for him. I only added a couple seeds. He's a lightweight."

The professor tasted my bowl. Waited for a reaction, and, when there was none, handed the bowl back. "Add salt and eat it slowly. You'll survive, but you will suffer when you..."

"I get the picture. I know how it feels the next day."

I managed to finish my stew by adding biscuits.

"Not bad, Joe," I handed him my empty bowl. "I might shoot you tomorrow though."

I retired to the Jeep, which was now back in its original location by the creek. Though the night was warm, I started a small fire hoping its light would help me read longer. I sat in the drier of the camp chairs and opened the journal. I had about ninety minutes to read before the sun would set. I leaned back, put my feet on the semi-flat rock I used as an ottoman and read the first page. At first I had trouble deciphering the partially faded handwriting, but after several attempts, I figured it out. I chuckled at the misspelled words, most of which could be corrected by a child in third grade.

On the third page I learned this was the journal of Gordie Hough, the oldest son of Bill Hough. He was born in 1860 and was seventeen years old when he wrote the journal. I surmised he wrote it while on a cattle drive to and from Sage Canyon in the late summer of 1877. He kept count of how many cattle were lost, either through illness or injury. Some were slaughtered to feed the men on the drive. He detailed the difficulties reaching the canyon floor. There was a crude drawing of the trail descending Piqua Mesa. I twisted my back until I could see where I had descended.

"No cattle will ever take that trail again."

I read more pages.

"Bandit, you should listen to this." I read aloud though Bandit was sleeping. "This was the ninth day after they had driven the cattle into the canyon. He mentions finding the mummified, partial carcasses of three burros. Nearby were the remains of several leather packs. He opened the packs, but all he found was powder and dust. He showed them to his father, who told him not to say anything to anyone." I stared at Bandit and called his name. He responded with a lifted ear. "Maybe Hough knew it was dust from the gold ore. What do you think, Bandit?" He exhaled and rolled over. "Well, it's more interesting than a law book."

I was fascinated by the entry several pages later. This was the first mention of a treasure and their search for the location of the mine. I turned the page hoping to learn the exact location, but two pages had been ripped out. "That sucks big time!"

The professor and Joe were returning from our new latrine and heard my exclamation.

"Did you get to the good part?" the professor asked.

"Do you think the treasure's location was on the missing pages?"

He nodded. "Why else remove them?"

"Who do you think did it? One of the Hough brothers, perhaps?"

"I once believed that, but if they had the location, why didn't they find the treasure?"

"Maybe they did." I sat up and took a drink of water.

"If they did, the family kept it a secret. I've searched through all printed references to the family." He shook his head. "There is no mention of it, and no evidence the family came into unexplained wealth."

I finished the journal and the treasure was mentioned two more times. In each case, at least one page was missing.

I stood, faced the professor and Joe and waved the journal at them. "Someone took the time to carefully read this and remove all the pages which might have disclosed a location."

"It's frustrating, huh?" the professor chuckled.

"Do you know what happened to the brothers, or their families?"

"I've done some investigating."

"Are you willing to share?" I asked to elicit a more detailed response.

"I know the older brother, Bill, left this area sometime in the 1890s and settled outside of Ouray, Colorado. He supposedly had become rather successful from the cattle business, and bought a large section of land on the southern side of Uncompahgre Mountain."

"What about the other brother?"

The professor stared at Joe. Joe stared back for a moment before turning his interest to a purple flower on one of the nearby Beavertail Prickly Pear plants.

"What?" I pointed menacingly at the men and tilted my head. "I know you're holding back. Spill it!"

Chapter Fourteen

⌐

The professor looked at me then at Ol' Joe.

Joe nodded and said, "Tell him what you know. It's not like it matters anymore. The entire family is gone. There are no living descendants in this world or the spirit world."

The professor glared at Joe. "Enough of your Native American spirit world. You only believe that when it suits you." He turned to me. "Okay, I'll explain what I know. Some of which is fact, but some is pure conjecture."

"Tell me. You've piqued my interest."

We sat facing each other. Joe stared into the fire.

"Do you see visions in the flames?"

"My grandfather could, but I didn't inherit that skill." He shrugged and added, "I like to watch the flames dancing and enjoy hearing the songs from the wood."

"No disrespect, Chief Joseph, but you are one seriously weird Native American."

The professor laughed, then said, "Each of the Hough brothers had two sons. This is common knowledge, and can be found in historical documents."

"That's not much help in finding the treasure," I replied after the professor paused.

"You have a journal from one son. He wrote about living in this canyon for a season."

"I imagine he must have returned and might have written more journals." I rubbed my hands together. "Now, if we could locate those journals, they might hold the answer."

"That sounds logical," the professor said.

"He might have stayed in Sage Canyon for years. He undoubtedly knew about the legend. He probably searched for the mine since he would have plenty of free time. It couldn't have been difficult to watch over a herd confined to this canyon."

The professor shook his head. "Didn't happen, unfortunately. He was killed two years later."

I checked the professor's eyes to make sure this was the truth. "How?"

"He was shot in the back after leaving a saloon in Chemical Creek, Idaho."

"Where's that?" I asked.

"It was a small mining camp in the central mountains outside of Columbia."

"Who shot him?"

The professor shrugged. "No one was ever charged with the crime, but the local sheriff, a man named O.V. Dill, did have two suspects. Men named Halbert and Sampson, who suddenly left town the next day. They turned up in Bedford Park, North Dakota a couple years later, but were destitute. They didn't have the treasure."

"Go on."

"The other brother moved to Canada for a time and was last heard of living somewhere in Alaska. I've never found evidence he had a family."

"Okay, that brings us to the other Hough brother. What was his name? I forgot."

"David. He was the younger brother. He left the area before his brother, and settled in Oregon. As far as anyone knows, he lived to old age though I've never found a death certificate. I never had any success tracing his sons, but they might have had families. It's all a mystery. The Hough name disappeared from public records in the early 1930s. No trace whatsoever. Totally gone. Poof!"

"I don't suppose there are other journals. Perhaps letters between family members?"

"What you have in your hands is all that exists. Any correspondence between the original brothers has been lost to time. You have to remember this was in the days before computers, emails and instant worldwide communication."

I laughed and pointed to the canyon wall. "Did we travel through time? We're in the same situation." I had forgotten about my satellite phone for the moment. I opened the journal. "The pages are numbered, but they don't start with page one. The first one is page fourteen. Several numbers are skipped, but it's not because of missing pages." I held it up to show them. "It's obvious where pages have been torn out, but the page numbers are weird."

"I did notice the discrepancy, but didn't assign it much credence," the professor said.

"Perhaps it's like that book *The Da Vinci Code*," Joe suggested. "We crack the code and find the treasure."

"Maybe the missing pages contained, not only, information about the mine's location, but a map as well," I said. "That would explain why someone removed them."

The professor shrugged. "Doesn't do us much good to speculate about what might have been on the missing pages. They are gone, and no wishful thinking will make them magically reappear."

"So, if we want to find the treasure, or the mine's location, we have to do it the old-fashioned way, huh?" I asked.

"What do you mean?"

"You've been investigating the canyon for the past forty years, right?"

He nodded.

"You kept a record of your explorations, correct?"

"Of course."

"And you are absolutely certain the mine wasn't found."

"Obviously."

"Have you searched the entire canyon from top to bottom?"

Joe and the professor stared at each other.

Joe laughed and said, "Do you really think the mine might have been located halfway up a vertical cliff? If so, the location would be visible."

I sighed and thought about that for a time. "Okay, point taken. My mistake. The mine could not be located where it was visible. It had to be camouflaged somehow."

"Are you sure you are really an attorney?" the professor asked.

Joe laughed.

"I still have my license to practice law. I could draw up your will and prepare... Never mind! I confess I'm out of my element. I wouldn't have the foggiest notion where to look for a goldmine."

"What do you intend to do with Zenus Sage, if that's who the skeleton is?" I asked after breakfast the next morning.

"Since I have no way of proving the skeleton's identity beyond all doubt, I intend to give it a proper burial."

Joe drained his coffee and said, "He was properly buried before you dug him up. I think you should return him to the ground where you found him."

"Other than his skull," the professor pointed to the cave, "his bones are still there."

"What can you prove about the skeleton?" I asked.

"Several things. The approximate age. The decade he died." He grinned at Joe and added, "He was a Caucasian male with a slight limp."

Joe rolled his eyes.

The professor continued, "He had red hair, blue eyes, enjoyed reading Gothic romance novels and loved to cook rabbits over a fire."

My jaw dropped. "Really? Are you pulling a Sherlock Holmes on me? Am I supposed to be Dr. Watson?"

The professor laughed. "I made up the last part. I have no clue about his eyes or hair, but I do know a little about his eating habits."

"How?"

"I've found the bones of small animals nearby, evidence of his fires, and the remains of a book. Part of the cover survived. *A Sicilian Romance* by Ann Radcliffe."

"Might have been his wife's book."

"There's no evidence of a wife or companion."

"Okay, I will give you that. How do you know he limped?"

He shrugged. "That was the easiest deduction. His right leg is shorter than his left. Thus, he had a slight limp."

Joe tapped his chin. "Unless he wore corrective shoes."

Chapter Fifteen

I made sure the campfire was totally out by dumping a bucket of red dirt on it. I coughed as some of the dust blew into my face. I walked a few steps to the Jeep, placed my hands on the ladder leading up to the rooftop tent and hesitated. I looked at Bandit, who was already in his bed under the ladder.

"I think I'll go for a walk. I need to clear my head. Care to join me?"

He understood the word *walk* and got to his feet. He wagged his tail and followed me into the darkness. The half-moon provided enough light for me to distinguish between the narrow trail and the vegetation and rocks on either side as I headed down the valley.

"Bandit, I never thought about stars and how amazing the night sky is in my former life. It's a shame I was so focused on a career I'm not sure I ever wanted."

I sat on a boulder, removed my St. Louis Cardinals baseball cap and ran a hand through my hair.

"Bandit, should I get it cut, or let it grow. I've never had long hair, but there isn't a barbershop in the valley, and I think I lost the scissors. It would sure surprise my parents if I came home with a ponytail."

I replaced my cap and gazed into the sky. Bandit sat patiently at my feet. I concentrated on the Milky Way and pondered my future once Bandit and I were able to leave Sage Canyon.

"Would you like to come back someday, Bandit?" I asked scratching his ears.

He didn't bark, but stared at me.

"I feel we've barely scratched the surface of the interesting places to explore. I made a list of places to visit, but I wonder how many, if any, of them will have as intriguing a story as Sage Canyon. We have skulls, skeletons and legends of lost treasure all in a setting that reminds me of a desert Garden of Eden."

Bandit tilted his head back and forth as I rambled for a time.

"Ready to head back?" I stood and Bandit trotted ahead of me. "Go ahead. You know the way back to camp better than I do."

I slept deeply through the night. It was still semi-dark when I climbed down the ladder to relieve myself. I listened to the sounds of the valley and chuckled.

"Bandit, whoever said it was quiet in nature must have lived in New York City their entire life. I made the mistake of assuming the nights would be quieter than the library at the firm's office." I chuckled and added, "It's downright noisy out here. How do you ever get any sleep?"

I must have jumped three feet off the ground when someone tapped my shoulder.

"Joe! What are you doing? You scared the rest of the crap out of me."

He put a finger to his lips and pointed to the top of the mesa.

"What? Is there someone stalking us?"

He led me to the opposite side of the clearing under the largest tree in the valley before answering, "I saw shadows up there."

I laughed and replied, "You can't see the tree behind us. How is it possible you saw shadows before the sun's fully up?"

"I saw them in my vision. Trust me. We are being observed."

"Does this have anything to do with the falling boulders?"

Joe nodded. "In my vision I could see the spirits of many people from the valley. They are unsettled."

"Why?" I asked when it became obvious he wasn't going to elaborate.

He grabbed my elbow and whispered, "It is because of the greed of people searching for the lost treasure."

"I don't suppose these spirits told you where the treasure is hidden, did they?"

He put his hands on my shoulders and stared into my eyes. "The spirits told me only a man with a pure heart will find the real treasure of Sage Canyon."

I stared in silence as he headed up the slope to the cave.

"Bandit, do you think Ol' Joe knows more than we do?"

He barked once.

"My feeling exactly."

"Did anything unusual wake you up during the night?" I asked the professor as I fried the last package of bacon a couple hours later.

"Unusual?" He shook his head. "I woke up because I'm an old man, and my bladder isn't what it used to be."

"I wasn't thinking of that."

"Other than getting up for... you know, I slept the deep sleep of a man at peace with the world."

"Are you turning into a philosopher?" I looked around. "Have you seen Joe? It's not like him to skip breakfast."

"No, I haven't seen him at all."

I told the professor about talking to Joe earlier.

"Yeah, he tells me about his visions. I usually attribute them to his spicy food."

"There could be something to it," I said. "Those boulders crashing close to us was no accident. I don't believe in coincidences."

I saw the professor later that afternoon and asked about Joe.

"I haven't seen him all day."

"Should we be worried? Could something have happened to him?"

"Perhaps, but he sometimes takes off without telling me. He might have gone to check on his special herbs. Let's not worry unless he doesn't return by tomorrow night."

Two days later Joe stumbled into camp and sat down heavily in a camp chair.

"Where have you been? Bandit and I spent most of yesterday looking for you. Are you hungry?"

"I wouldn't refuse something to eat."

"I'll fix some pasta. I was going to make it for supper anyway. While I'm doing that, you can tell me where you were."

The professor heard us talking and joined us. I opened the back of the Jeep, folded down the metal shelf and set up my kitchen.

"I'm listening," I said to Joe.

"Because of the vision I told you about, I decided to go off alone and seek a deeper experience..."

The professor interrupted with a snort. "You mean you were smoking more of your loco weed, right?"

"It clears my mind, so I can fully understand my visions."

"You're lucky the government doesn't know about its *medicinal* purposes, or else they would make it illegal."

"You didn't tell us where you were." I broke the spaghetti in half and added it to the pot. "We were concerned you might have been injured."

"I checked on... my special garden."

"Told you so," the professor interrupted again.

"I needed to tend to them. Then I spent a night on my secret ledge."

"Where is that?"

Joe stared silently at me.

The professor laughed and said, "Secret ledge my butt! Twenty or thirty years ago he found this ledge above the lake. He goes there to get away from me. Especially if I need him to do some work. He thinks I don't know where he goes."

"I found a ledge above the lake. I've been there a few times."

Joe jumped up and pointed a finger at me. "I could feel your presence on my ledge. The spirits told me an outsider had been there."

I laughed and said, "Spirits, huh? Maybe it was the energy bar wrapper I left behind."

Chapter Sixteen

⚒

"Bandit and I will be gone most of the day. Don't worry about us. I have my backpack with plenty of food and water." I hoisted the heavier than usual pack onto my back and adjusted the straps. "Ready to head out, Bandit?"

Bandit barked and took off with his nose to the trail. I noticed the professor and Joe watching as we left camp.

"Hiram, didn't you say something about Rhett having a satellite phone?"

"Yes," the professor nodded. "He said he bought it because it doesn't rely on cell towers. It uses satellites and is never out of reach. He can always get in touch with people."

"Have you ever used one?"

"I don't think I've ever seen one. Why?"

Joe gazed at the mesa rim. "I think we should get in touch with the sheriff's department because of everything that's happened lately. The boulders falling off the mesa. The unexplained feeling of being watched..."

"Are you getting paranoid, Joe?"

"Is it paranoia if there really is someone watching you?"

The professor shrugged. "I'm an archaeologist not a philosophy professor."

Joe rolled his eyes then started walking toward the Jeep. "Where does he keep it?"

The professor followed Joe toward the Jeep. "Either in his backpack, which he has with him, or in the Jeep. What are you thinking?"

Joe opened the driver's door. "Where would you put an expensive phone?"

"Probably under the seat where it would be out of sight, but still handy in case of an emergency."

"I think we have an emergency situation on our hands," Joe said reaching under the seat. He pulled out a brown case and showed it to the professor. "I do believe this might be it."

"Maybe we should think about this. We might need a password to use it."

"Maybe," Joe said unzipping the case.

"Didn't your ancestors teach you how to use smoke signals to communicate?"

"Yes, but that was a long time ago. I could send a signal, but whoever sees it probably wouldn't know how to decipher it."

The professor sighed. "Even if they couldn't understand the signal, they could see the smoke and connect that to a fire. They would call the fire department, or the police. Is there a special signal to use to call for help?"

Joe shrugged as he looked at the buttons on the phone. "To be perfectly honest, all I know about smoke signals is to use wet wood. It makes a lot of smoke."

"There had to be different signals."

"I don't know any classified signals my people used. We didn't use Morse code."

"Some chief you are," the professor sighed.

"There are a bunch of buttons on the front, but I'm afraid to touch them."

"Give it to me," the professor ordered. He inspected the phone, turned it over then checked the buttons on the side. "Aha!"

"What is it? What did you find? Do you know how to use it?"

"I'm not sure, but do you see this?" He held the phone to let Joe see it.

"I see it."

The professor rolled his eyes. "It looks just like the power button on my cell phone."

"Wait a minute. What if it sends a signal to some satellite halfway around the globe. How would we explain where we are?"

"Don't know. Don't care." The professor pressed the button.

"Did you press it?"

"Yes, but nothing's happening."

"Is the phone already turned on?"

"How should I know?"

"Give it to me."

The professor handed it back to Joe, who stared at it.

"Well, is it on or not?"

"I think this screen would be showing something if it was turned on."

"Well, turn it on. Press the power button again."

"Which one is it? There are several buttons."

"Keep pressing them until the darn thing powers up."

"Okay, but if we break this thing, I'm telling Rhett it was your idea and your fault."

Joe pressed two buttons. The professor turned away and shielded his face with his arm.

"Did it power up?" the professor asked.

"Nothing. Nada. Zilch." Joe looked at the professor and laughed. "It's not a bomb, and holding your arm like that wouldn't protect you if it was."

"Try the button I showed you."

Joe pushed the correct button until the screen glowed.

"Got it."

"Dial 9-1-1."

"This is a phone, right? What if I dial the sheriff's office directly?"

"Why do you know the sheriff's phone number?"

Joe hesitated to answer.

"Answer me!"

"He's dating my daughter," Joe admitted.

"Snowflower?"

Joe shook his head. "He's dating the younger one. Moonbeam."

"Since when? Is it serious?"

"Don't ask." He dialed the number and waited. "There will be a new warrior in the family soon."

"That sounds pretty serious."

"Ya think?"

"Is it ringing?"

"I think so."

"How can I help you?" a voice asked startling Joe and the professor. Joe lost his hold on the phone and it fell to the ground.

"Now you've done it." The professor shook his head. "You put it on speaker mode."

Joe picked up the phone.

"How can I help you?"

"Tell them who we are, and where we are." The professor tried to grab the phone from Joe.

Joe swatted the professor's hands away. "Back away, Talks Too Much, and let me handle this."

"Fine."

"Uh, yes," Joe cleared his throat, held the phone at arm's length and spoke slowly, "This is Chief Joseph Paledeer of the..."

Eventually, the sheriff came on the line.

"Joe? Is that really you? Is Moonbeam all right?"

"Yes it is. I hate to bother you, however..."

Ten minutes later, all the pertinent information had been passed along.

"I will contact the highway department, and light a fuse under their butts. Is there anything else I can do?"

Joe looked at the professor, who shook his head. "I think we're okay for now."

"I feel safer already," the professor said. "Did you turn it off? Should we let Rhett know we used his phone? He probably has to pay for every call."

"You can tell him." Joe replaced the phone in its case and shoved it under the seat. "He may never know if we don't mention it."

"I will tell him when he and Bandit return."

"Are they playing prospector again?"

"He wanted to search a few places. I hope he doesn't get hurt climbing the cliffs."

"Hold on a minute. I can hear Bandit barking," the professor said long after dark. He and Joe were sitting in the camp chairs by the fire trying to one-up each other by telling the most fantastic tales.

A moment later Bandit bounded into the clearing. He ran excitedly back and forth between the professor and Ol' Joe wagging his tail frantically.

"Are you trying to tell us something, Bandit? Where is Rhett? Is he hurt? Do we need to rescue him?"

"Show us where he is," Joe said getting out of his chair. "Lead the way, Bandit."

I hobbled into camp before they could set out on a search and rescue mission. Bandit raced back to me.

"We were getting ready to search for you," Joe said.

"Without flashlights?"

"We were hoping you would be close," the professor said. "Did you hurt your ankle?"

"Twisted it a bit on a slippery boulder. It's okay. Anything happen while I was gone? Oh, I didn't find any treasure in case you were curious."

Joe looked at the professor.

"You tell him," the professor insisted.

"No, you do it."

I held up my hands. "Stop! Someone tell me what happened."

Joe cleared his throat and confessed.

"How did you bypass the password?"

The men shrugged.

I rubbed my jaw and shifted my weight to my uninjured ankle. "Never mind. Maybe I left it unlocked."

"We put it back."

"I was going to use smoke signals, but Talks Too Much insisted we use your fancy phone."

The professor shook a fist at him.

"I didn't find the treasure, but I did find this." I opened my backpack and pulled out what I had found.

The professor and Joe stared without speaking.

"Aren't you curious about what I found?" I yelled after hearing their silence for a time.

The professor nodded. "Yes. Show us."

"I am! This is what I found." I held it out to let them see it easier.

Joe squinted and edged closer. "What is it?"

"I don't think a Coke can is exactly the legendary treasure."

I waved it at them. "This is evidence. We are being watched."

"By someone on the rim who drinks Coke?" the professor asked.

"Maybe, but I found this can at the edge of the creek."

"Of course," Joe muttered.

I added, "Someone must have left it there. That means they are in the canyon. It's unopened..."

"Please tell me you aren't going to drink it." The professor made a face.

"Don't you think it odd to find an unopened can of Coke in Sage Canyon?"

"Not at all." Joe seized the can from me, popped it open and took a long drink. "I left it there to stay cold, but then I forgot where I put it. Thanks for bringing it back to camp."

Chapter Seventeen

I rested my injured ankle for two days. Then Bandit and I returned to the far western end of the canyon. I climbed onto the same ledge above the lake and watched the same fish swimming aimlessly in the clear water. I thought about the professor's nugget.

"Bandit, I would swear in a court of law on a stack of bibles the professor found that nugget at the same time he found the skull of Zenus Sage, or whoever it might be."

Bandit sat beside me. I scratched his ears, and he closed his eyes and promptly fell asleep.

"I don't suppose it makes any difference where he found it. He obviously didn't find the lost mine, but I'm totally convinced a mine of some size exists here in the canyon. Maybe no one has found it because they've all been searching for something large and obvious. Perhaps the mine was much smaller, and people have been looking at it for years without seeing it for what it was."

I decided to stop talking to myself, climbed off the ledge, made my way to the cool water, stripped out of my dusty clothes and walked into the lake. Bandit barked once from the ledge, but lay back down and resumed his nap. I shivered until I adjusted to the cold water. Then I floated on my back from one side of the lake to the other letting my mind wander freely about nothing in particular.

I don't know how long I was in the lake, but I eventually walked out. I soaked my clothes in the water and even rubbed them on a rock like I had seen Native Americans do in a Hollywood movie. I spread them out in the sun to let them dry. I looked at my body and laughed at my farmer's tan.

"Bandit, are you there? Are you still sleeping?"

He stood and barked.

"Look! My arms and legs are browner than I can ever remember, while the rest of my body is whiter than the clouds." I pointed to the sky. "They float lazily across the sky teasing us with the possibility of a rain they seldom provide."

He lay back down, rolled over a couple times then ignored me.

My clothes were still partially wet when I got dressed. I knew the afternoon sun would soon dry them completely. I took a different track as I headed back. I stayed as close as possible to the north canyon wall. In some places I had to scramble over boulders, some as large as my Jeep. I had become fitter than ever since I began my overlanding journey. The miles of hiking and climbing in Sage Canyon strengthened my body and re-energized my mind. For the first time since the day I descended into the canyon from Piqua Mesa, I thought about finding the slot canyon and escaping. I shielded the sun with my hand and gazed across the valley at Escape Canyon.

"I need to be patient. I wouldn't get far without the Jeep."

I thought about Ol' Joe's horse and wondered if Flies Over Clouds was back home waiting patiently for his owner. Bandit woke from his most recent nap and joined me. I rubbed his ears as he wagged his tail.

"Would you wait for me if... oh, never mind."

We continued to explore this section of the canyon. I came across different, and possibly unique, varieties of cacti and wildflowers.

"Noura loved flowers," I whispered.

Bandit barked once when he heard her name. He spotted three does and a buck, but they ignored us, and he ignored them. He jumped into the creek at one point. I wasn't sure if he was trying to catch a fish for supper, or simply cooling off. I called for him to come back, but he decided to return to camp by way of the creek. I didn't blame him.

I found the hot air balloon again and chuckled at the thought of flying out of the canyon. I gazed at the top of the canyon walls remembering the day the boulders crashed down. It might have been a trick of the light, but, for a fraction of a second, I thought I saw someone leaning out over the edge and looking down at me. I blinked and the image vanished.

"I was talking to myself earlier, and now I'm seeing things. Must be the seeds Joe adds to his stew."

No boulders crashed down the cliff. I kept going and resisted the temptation to climb a narrow crack in the wall. I was no longer terrified of heights, but I sure didn't want to get stuck and have to wait for a rescue that might never arrive.

I kept hiking as close to the bottom of the cliff as possible and eventually reached the waterfall. I understood why the professor thought this had to be the location of the mine.

"Bandit, we need to return later this week to do more exploring."

I wasn't sure if he agreed with my plan or not. He didn't bark at all.

I decided to return to the waterfall after breakfast. I explained how hard I would be working to Bandit, and gave him the choice of going with me, or staying with the professor and Joe. He chose to stay in camp where there was shade.

"He's all yours," I said to them. "Don't spoil him too much."

"If he's smart, he will take a nap like we plan on doing," Joe said.

"All he does is eat and take naps."

"I knew he was smarter than the average dog," Joe said while scratching Bandit's ear.

I borrowed the professor's tools and eagerly set about searching for the mine. I knew I didn't have to look in the places the professor had searched, so that eliminated several areas.

I knew how to use a shovel because of Noura's love of gardening. I had never swung a pickaxe in my life, but I soon got the hang of it and didn't stab myself in the foot. I gained a new respect for the miners I had read about and saw in movies.

After three hours of hard labor, I sat on a boulder with sweat pouring off my body in rivers and ignored the snake that slithered past. My clothes were soaked from both my exertion and the refreshing spray from the falls. I wiped my face with my bandana, took a long drink of warm water and listened to the water crashing behind me.

"Why am I drinking this when the waterfall is cool and clear?"

I emptied my bottle and refilled it with the cold water from the spring.

Ten minutes later I was back at work. I was grateful for the loan of the professor's thick work gloves. Otherwise, my hands would be raw and quite painful later.

By the end of the afternoon, I had created more piles of dirt than the professor's previous labor. I moved boulders in the creek and worried I might change its course, or dam it and create another flood. The creek continue on its course without registering my presence.

"Any luck?" the professor asked as I wandered into camp.

I shook my head and slumped into the empty camp chair beside him.

He handed me a bottle of water. "We will find it eventually." He smiled slyly, and I wondered if he actually believed his words.

Chapter Eighteen

⼉

The doorbell rang three times. Stopped. Then four more rapid rings.

"It must be the UPS driver. Hiram's package is supposed to come today. Just be a minute," Effie Hirschfield said to the neighbor as she set her coffee cup on the kitchen table. She dried her hands on a dish towel, smoothed out her apron and made her way to the front door. She stopped to straighten one of the photos of her grandchildren on the wall in the hallway. "Hold on! I'm coming," She pulled the heavy door open, put a hand to her breast and said, "You're not who I expected to see."

"I didn't mean to startle you," the man said. "Can I come in?"

"Of course." She stepped aside to let Officer Gordon enter.

He removed his hat and asked, "Is the professor home?"

She shook her head. "He's been in the canyon for several weeks."

"I thought that might be the case."

"Is he okay? Do you have bad news?"

"No, ma'am. I do need to ask if you've seen this man." He pulled a photo from a folder and showed it to her. "Have you seen this man recently, or ever?"

She reached for her glasses which were dangling on a chain around her neck. "Let me take a look."

Officer Gordon handed her the 8x10 photo, glanced down the hallway and listened for sounds revealing something might be amiss.

"Are you alone? Is someone here?"

"My neighbor Ardith is here. We were drinking coffee and talking about the neighbors. We are such gossips," she tittered.

"The photo, please."

She handed it back after a quick look. "He was here just after Hiram left for Utah. Is there a problem? Who is he? He seemed like a nice young man. He claimed to be a former student."

"Did he mention his name?"

"Not that I recall. That's strange now that you ask."

"Did he ask where the professor was, or how soon he would be returning?"

Effie lowered her glasses as she thought about the question. "I got the feeling he knew the location of Sage Canyon. I assumed he might have been on one of the archaeological expeditions." She looked up at the officer. "Scott, you're frightening me. Should I try to call Hiram? He doesn't usually have cell reception in the canyon, but I could send a text. He might receive that sooner or later."

"You can keep this copy. We have others."

She took the photo back as Officer Gordon pulled a wrinkled sheet of paper from the folder. "This came from the man's motel room. One of the maids found it in the garbage can. It had been wadded up. I think he might have intended to give it to you but changed his mind."

"What does it say?"

Officer Gordon summarized the note for her. "He claims to be descended from the Hough family who lived in the Sage Canyon a long time ago."

"I know the name, but Hiram said the family disappeared almost a hundred years ago."

"This letter claims he is the rightful owner of some kind of treasure. Gold. Silver. Whatever. He claims the professor is in possession of the gold, or at least knows its location." He looked at Mrs. Hirschfield again. "I'm sorry, but he makes some threats."

"You know Hiram has been searching for the lost Zenus Sage mine for years, but has never found it. I always believed it was a myth until a couple years ago."

"Would you call us if he comes back? We don't think he's dangerous, and he hasn't committed a crime as far as we know. We would like to talk to him though."

"I understand. I'll call you if I see him, or if I hear from Hiram."

He replaced his hat and backed away. "I'd appreciate it, ma'am."

"Say hello to your lovely wife for me, and tell Patricia she should bring Gina over sometime. She should resume her piano lessons."

"I will."

Effie stood at the door and waited until Officer Gordon drove away. She looked at the photo again as she headed back to the kitchen.

"Who was at the door?" Ardith asked. "It wasn't the UPS driver."

"Officer Gordon. They are looking for this man." She showed the photo to Ardith.

"He looks sinister."

"He was here after Hiram left. I thought he was nice." Effie explained what the young man wanted, and what was written in the note.

"I hope it's just a misunderstanding."

"I should take a picture of this with my cell phone and forward it to Hiram."

"Yes! Right away," Ardith insisted. "If you can't figure out how to do it, Ben from next door can do it for you. He's only a child, but he knows how to use modern technology."

The professor's cell phone chimed, and he pulled it from his back pocket and smiled. "I just received a text from Effie. I haven't been able to get a signal all week. I wonder what she's up to. I should read it."

"Tell her hello for me," Joe said.

"I'm surprised you can get cell reception in the canyon."

"It's rare."

"I gave up waiting for a signal."

"Sometimes the atmospheric conditions are just right and there is a weak signal. It usually coincides with rain. I hope we're not in for another afternoon storm," the professor said.

"Yes, I can smell it approaching. Are you going to read the text, or stand there yapping your jaw?" Ol' Joe asked.

"All right! I'm reading it."

We were standing in the clearing about thirty feet from where I had moved the Jeep. I opened a bottle of water and was about to take a drink when something thudded into the dirt somewhere to my left. A split-second later we heard the sound.

"What was that?" I dropped the bottle of water.

The professor looked up at the mesa. "Get down!" he screamed. "That was a gunshot."

Chapter Nineteen

⌐

We took cover behind the nearby boulders. Several more shots rang out over the next couple minutes.

"Who is shooting at us?" I yelled at the professor. "How many are there? Can you tell?"

The professor stuffed his cell phone into his back pocket after reading Effie's text, peeked over his boulder and studied the top of Piqua Mesa. "It could be three or four men, but my gut tells me it's only one."

"But the shots came from different areas."

"I think he's taking a shot then moving to give us an impression of strength in numbers."

"He's moving pretty fast."

We ducked under cover as another shot ricocheted off the rocks in front of us.

Joe yelled and grabbed his bicep.

"He's been hit!"

The professor scrambled closer and took a look at Joe's arm.

"Will he be okay?" I asked.

"He will survive. It's just a flesh wound. A mere scratch from the rock."

"That's easy for you to say," Joe said wincing with pain. "It's my time. I feel it in my bones."

"Quit bellyaching." The professor looked at me and said, "Let me have your shirt."

"Why? He can't be cold."

"I need something to wrap around his arm, and I'm wearing my lucky shirt."

I understood the request now. I removed my one decent shirt and was down to a Fridays At Five t-shirt.

"I'll sacrifice it for the cause."

The professor wrapped Joe's arm with the strips of my shirt.

"That should stop the bleeding."

"It will take more than one wound to finish me," Joe said.

Another shot rang out echoing off the canyon walls.

"I'm hit again. This is the end of the line for me. I will soon join my ancestors."

The professor checked Joe out.

"You haven't been hit again. You aren't joining your ancestors until I send you there."

We heard another shot, and cringed. But we couldn't tell where it landed. There was no sound of it hitting anything nearby.

"Whoever is shooting has worse aim than Ol' Joe," the professor said.

"All it takes is one lucky shot," I said. "Remember how Joe's arrow hit my Jeep?"

"The spirits of my ancestors guided the arrow to your Jeep," Joe whispered. "Let's hope the shooter's not in touch with his ancestors."

We crouched as low as we could behind the rocks.

"I wish we were behind the Jeep," Joe said.

It was then I remembered my sat-phone.

"We could scatter simultaneously. He couldn't shoot all of us if we run in different directions," I said.

"One in three," the professor said. "I don't like those odds."

We stayed put. There were no more shots for several minutes.

"Do you think they've given up? Did the shooters leave?" Joe asked.

The question was answered as something landed in the rocks fifty feet in front of us. A split-second later, the area exploded.

"What was that?" I asked as dirt, rocks and vegetation flew in all directions.

"I think the shooter has chosen a new tactic," the professor said.

Joe nodded. "Dynamite."

"He's going to blow us up?" I asked incredulously.

"It would be easier than shooting us unless he's a trained sniper."

The next explosion took place a hundred feet above the canyon floor with little effect other than making a loud bang.

I asked, "Is he trying to adjust the fuse, or something?"

"I'm no expert on explosives, but I suggest we move to the cave."

We decided to scatter and head for the cave.

"On the count of three."

They nodded.

"One..."

Joe dashed away, and the professor followed. I shook my head.

"So much for my countdown."

I glanced at the top of the mesa. When I didn't see or hear anything, I followed them up the slope to the cave.

"We'll be safe in here," the professor said as we tried to catch our breath and force our hearts to resume a normal pace.

We sat motionless for several minutes. Then Joe stepped to the edge of the cave and looked up. "Hiram, couldn't he drop a stick of dynamite down the opening and blow us to smithereens?"

The professor slapped his forehead then answered, "That's true, but it will take him time to get to this side of the mesa."

"I don't plan to wait until he arrives," I said. "We need to be proactive."

"What are you going to do?" Joe asked. He glanced at the bandage on his arm and saw the blood seeping through. "I'm mortally wounded."

The professor tore another strip from my shirt and replaced the blood-soaked bandage.

"There! You'll be okay. The blood has stopped flowing." He looked at me and asked his question again.

"My sat-phone is in the Jeep. Your cell phone might be useless, but I can call for help."

"Go for it. I think we have a window of safety while whoever's out there decides on a new course of action."

"I sure hope you're right, professor." I looked at Bandit. "Stay here and guard everyone. I'll be back in a flash."

"Poor choice of words," Joe said.

I took a quick peak at the top of the mesa where I thought the last shot came from. "I think it's safe."

"At least it's all downhill to the Jeep," the professor said.

I took a deep breath and dashed from the cave. I made it several feet before the rocks gave way, and I fell. I tumbled most of the way down the slope without suffering anything more serious than the loss of skin on my hands, arms and knees.

"Are you okay!" the professor hollered.

"Just flesh wounds." The back of my t-shirt was ripped to shreds.

I stayed low and made it to the Jeep without further incident. I pulled on the driver's door. "Crap! Why did I lock it?"

Chapter Twenty

"What's wrong?" the professor yelled.

"I locked the Jeep last night. Stupid habit, I know. The keys are in the backpack in the cave."

"I'll get them." He disappeared and returned shortly. "I'll throw them to you."

"Wait!"

Too late. The professor threw the keys. I watched them sail over the Jeep and swore under my breath.

"Sorry!"

I sat with my back to the Jeep and waved. "It's not your fault." I thought about the spare set. I realized I had hidden the second key fob under a boulder at the base of a cactus ten feet from rear of the Jeep. Then I remembered the flash flood. "I hope it's still there." I scooted to the rear tire.

We heard the bullet hit the passenger side of the Jeep before we heard the gun fire.

"This isn't going to be easy."

I got to a crouch, waited for the next shot. When it thudded harmlessly into the dirt fifty feet away, I sprinted for the boulder. I used both hands to furiously scoop out the dirt.

"I found the spare keys!" I yelled as I dashed back to the relative safety of the Jeep.

"Great! Open the door. Grab the phone and get back here."

I opened the door as the rear passenger window shattered. I reached under the seat, blindly searching for the satellite phone, as the firing continued. I touched it and discovered it was wedged in place. I tugged with the extra strength provided by the adrenaline coursing through my body. It came free. I powered it up and punched in the number. It rang three times.

"Rhett, I'm glad you called. Your mother..."

"Dad! You need to listen..."

Two minutes later he came back on the line. "I relayed your position to the authorities, but it might take them a while to reach you."

"Thanks, Dad, but I'm not sure we have much time left." I ended the call.

Another shot rang out echoing off the canyon walls.

"Like I said before, this guy is a worse shot than Ol' Joe," the professor hollered. "That hit a tree twenty yards in front of the creek."

"All it takes is one lucky shot," I said. "He hit the window."

The gunman appeared to be taking a break. Then he decided to alternate between firing his gun and tossing sticks of dynamite to the canyon floor. I looked at the professor and, to my shock, saw a black streak emerge from the safety of the cave.

"Bandit! Go back!" I screamed as I watched him racing down the slope.

"Bandit! Come back," Joe yelled.

He reached my side, and I pulled him to the ground. His tail was wagging, but I could see a look of terror in his eyes. "You should have stayed with Joe and the professor." He licked my face and barked... twice.

The gunman must have been running low on ammunition because he only fired every couple of minutes. I could hear the bullets hit, but none of them came close to us. Bandit stayed next to me even when he spotted two rabbits sitting under a cactus.

I put my hands over my head when I heard the next explosion though I knew that wouldn't protect me. I closed my eyes and thought about Noura and Reid.

"God, if you're there, and this is my time, I sure would like to see my family again. I will never understand why they were taken from me, but I guess You must have known something I don't."

Bandit sat on my legs, licked my face, and I could feel his tail thumping on my legs. Just like he used to do with Reid.

The next explosion sounded much farther away than the others. A few seconds later I heard the sound of rocks falling from the cliff.

"I think that came from the top of the mesa, and I don't hear any more gunfire, Bandit. Maybe he ran out of bullets."

Bandit barked... several times.

Are you all right?" the professor asked from behind the large boulder near the cave entrance. He and Joe slowly made their way down the slope toward the Jeep. "Did you see what happened?"

"I didn't see it, but I heard an explosion. It might have come from on top of the mesa. Do you know what happened?"

"I believe our shooter lit a short fuse, tossed it over the edge, but must have lost his footing. Or maybe the explosion caused it. But regardless. He won't be a danger anymore."

"Why?"

"You didn't see him fall?"

"No. I didn't see anything. I heard rocks falling. I closed my eyes, and said a quick prayer."

"He fell from the mesa. Not sure where he landed, but no one could survive such a fall. I doubt if there's much left of the body."

The professor and Ol' Joe reached us. He checked to make sure I was okay.

"I'm not hurt," I said. "Shaken up, but not injured other than the scrapes I sustained when I tumbled down the slope earlier."

"That was some tumbling exhibition," Joe said with a smile. "I'm glad the spirits spared you. They would probably give you a perfect score."

The dust settled, and we cautiously moved from our position of safety. Bandit raced ahead and discovered the body first. He was now standing guard over it. We couldn't be sure the shooter was acting alone, so we kept looking to the rim, ready to drop at the slightest sound from above.

"Good boy, Bandit. Let's see if we can identify him."

The body was face down in the dirt. The arms and legs were obviously broken and blood darkened the red dirt around him. The professor and I turned him over as Joe acted as lookout.

"I'm surprised the face is relatively undamaged. Can't say the same for the rest of him though."

"Do you recognize him?" I asked the professor after we had a chance to study his face.

The professor sighed, closed his eyes for a moment before nodding.

"Who is he?"

"He used the name Tom Carrier when he was in one of my classes."

"I take it that's not his real name."

"His real name is... excuse me... was... Tom Hough."

I eyed the professor then stared at the lifeless body in front of us. "I thought you said there was no one left."

"I was wrong."

"Well, there might not be any descendants left now."

Joe would not look at the body, but he asked, "Why do you remember this man? You had many students over the years. How can you be certain of his identity?"

"He has a small scar above his right eye."

Joe motioned for me to take a look. He still would not glance at the deceased. I checked for the scar.

"Okay, the scar is there, but barely visible. It's not enough to make an identification."

"Effie texted me, and I saw it just before the shooting started. She sent a photo with the text."

He pulled up the photo on his phone and showed it to me. I compared the photo to the face on the ground.

"I'd say this is the man in the photo."

"I agree," the professor said.

"What did the text say?"

He handed me his phone and let me read it for myself.

I read it twice and stared at the photo until the image was burned into my memory before handing the phone back to the professor.

"Just because he claimed to be descended from the Hough family doesn't make it true. If he is who he claims, where has he been all these years? How is he related? Why did he choose this time to..."

"We may never know the answers, but I don't think he really intended to kill us. I think he was trying to chase us out of the canyon."

"He was shooting at us," I reminded the professor.

"Yes, but I believe he hit everything he aimed for."

The professor brushed away some red dust from the deceased's right arm and said, "This tattoo is rather unique."

I leaned closer.

"I've never seen a tattoo like that before."

"I caught a brief glimpse of it in class one day."

I stared at the tattoo of a marble-sized golden nugget.

An hour later we were talking by the Jeep when the professor grabbed my arm.

"Do you hear that?"

We stopped talking and Bandit perked up his ears.

"It sounds like a helicopter."

We looked in every direction.

"The echoes make it impossible to tell where it's coming from," the professor said.

Joe put his hands behind his ears. He listened for a few seconds, turned to the east and pointed. "It's coming from there."

A short time later I spotted the chopper coming from the west and pointed to it.

The professor smacked Joe's arm. "Some help you are."

He shrugged and replied, "Maybe the pilot got lost."

When the helicopter was close enough, we waved frantically. The pilot spotted us. It didn't land, but turned sideways and hovered fifty feet, or so, above the canyon floor. We covered our ears as three armed men rappelled down ropes. They raced to our location, and we explained what had happened.

"The pilot is looking for a place to land. Does anyone need emergency medical treatment? We can airlift you to the hospital."

"We are all right, but there was one casualty."

"A man fell from the top of Piqua Mesa," the professor said.

Three hours later the helicopter left the canyon with the body of Tom Hough. The professor used the sat-phone and talked to his wife. He told her everyone was okay. I called my father to thank him. I talked to my mother, and, of course, she insisted I return home immediately. I pretended to have technical issues and ended the call.

"I have no idea how much that thing cost, but it was worth every bit of gold dust you paid," Joe said.

I laughed and replied, "I didn't use gold dust. I used plastic."

"I don't know about the rest of you," the professor said, "but my stomach is growling, and I think Bandit just found something for supper."

He pointed and Bandit dropped his latest catch at Joe's feet. He had learned how to fish.

Chapter Twenty-One

> ⟋

A week after the death of Tom Hough, my time in Sage Canyon was coming to an end. I spent the entire morning cleaning out the Jeep, taking a thorough inventory and then reloading it. The professor and Joe helped by sitting in my camp chairs, watching and offering advice. Bandit took a nap on the ground between them.

"Okay, I'm all packed. Thanks ever so much for your help."

The professor nudged Joe and whispered, "I do believe the lawyer is being facetious."

"I'm glad you're finished." Joe stood and patted his stomach. "I'm hungry enough to eat some of Talks Too Much's cooking."

The professor made another rabbit stew. Joe added some of his secret spices. I made the biscuits including an extra one for Bandit. We sat in the clearing by the creek to eat.

"Do you think your Jeep will make it up the new trail?" the professor asked. He pointed toward the western end of the canyon then gazed at the top of the thousand foot high walls of Sage Canyon.

"It's never failed me yet," I answered. "Please thank your friends from the county for reconstructing a road."

"I will."

Joe surprised us by offering to clean up after lunch.

"You're a good influence on him, Rhett. He's never once volunteered to clean up in all the time I've known him."

"Talks Too Much is losing his memory," Joe said. "I cleaned up twice... ten years ago."

I checked my campsite for the third time.

"Don't worry," the professor said. "If you leave anything behind, I keep it in the ruin with Zenus Sage's bones."

"That's why I'm triple-checking."

"Did you put his skull back where it belongs?" Joe asked.

The professor nodded.

"Okay, I'm ready."

I made a show of unlocking the Jeep to tease the guys. Then climbed inside.

"Here goes nothing."

I pushed the start button, and it fired to life. I checked the gas gauge. I still had half a tank. I got out and Bandit jumped in. I walked to where the professor and Ol' Joe waited to say goodbye.

I faced Ol' Joe. His expression remained stoic as if he were made of stone.

"How is your arm?"

He put a hand on the wound. "I do not feel pain. I am a proud warrior."

I smiled.

He held out his arms.

We embraced.

"You're going to be a grandfather soon. Will you teach your grandson the old ways?"

He shook his head. "I can't remember enough of them to make it worthwhile. But I might teach him how to handle a bow and arrow."

I turned to face the professor, and clenched my jaw to bolster my courage. I tried to think of something profound to say, but had a brain cramp.

I exhaled and said, "I'll blast the horn when I make it to the top."

He nodded, and I saw sadness in his eyes.

I couldn't make up my mind how to say goodbye, so I shook hands with the professor.

He pulled me close and bear-hugged me without a comment.

I backed away and said, "I'm sorry we didn't find the treasure."

For six days we searched continuously without any success other than uncovering a few pieces of broken pottery and several arrowheads.

"What would I do had we found it?" the professor asked with a shrug. "My quest in life is to search the past for truth and knowledge... and the occasional artifact."

I nodded because I understood now. It had taken an entire month in Sage Canyon, but now I understood.

"You were right about something you said when we first met, Professor."

"What might that be?" he asked though the twinkle in his eyes revealed he knew exactly what I meant.

"I do still believe in God."

He smiled, rubbed his beard and I saw a small puff of dust.

I turned, walked back to the Jeep and got in. Bandit sat on his haunches in the passenger seat and tried to lick my face.

"Are we ready for our next adventure?"

He barked. One bark only.

That was when I noticed the nugget in the cup holder.

Check out these other titles by the author.
Visit the website:
kennethleemcgee.com

The Emmy's Story Series

1. We Were 'posed to Get Married
2. One Of The Guys
3. A New Friend
4. Did You Like the Ravioli Tonight?
5. Completely and Forever: A Wedding
6. It's Time To Go!
7. How Difficult Can It Be?
8. Forever... Isabella... Forever
9. The Forgettable Year
10. Turning Thirty
11. Hello, I'm James
12. Remember The Struggle
13. But God! I Write Songs
14. A Lifelong Dream
15. Gideon's Tree
16. New Priorities
17. Christmas Surprise
18. God Is In Control
19. Life Goes On
20. Change Is Good

The Annie Mercer O'Dell Series

1. Roosevelt High
2. North Park College
3. Smoky Mountain Summer

The Stockton Woods Series

1. Sounds Like a Mournful Train Today
2. Sounds Like a Happy Train Today
3. Sounds Like a Cheerful Train Today

The Rex Ford & Clay Horn Books

1. The Amazing Adventures Of Rex Ford & Clay Horn

Stand Alone Books

1. Growing Up In Kinmundy Junction
2. Grandpa, Lions and Kitty Cats: A Collection Of Short Stories For Children Of All Ages
3. The True Stories Of Ol' Melvin, Obadiah, Perkins MacGhee and other Characters
4. Grandpa, Lions and More Kitty Cats: A Second Collection Of Short Stories For Children Of All Ages
5. Random Thoughts of a Strange Mind